OVERDRIVE

An L.T. Stafford Novel, No Copycat

D.Michael Day

Overdrive
Copyright © 2022 by D.Michael Day

All rights reserved. No part of this publication may be reproduced, distributed, or transmitted in any form or by any means, including photocopying, recording, or other electronic or mechanical methods, without the prior written permission of the author, except in the case of brief quotations embodied in critical reviews and certain other non-commercial uses permitted by copyright law.

Tellwell Talent
www.tellwell.ca

ISBN
978-0-2288-8687-7 (Hardcover)
978-0-2288-8686-0 (Paperback)
978-0-2288-8688-4 (eBook)

TABLE OF CONTENTS

Chapter One 1
Chapter Two 5
Chapter Three 10
Chapter Four 13
Chapter Five 18
Chapter Six 21
Chapter Seven 30
Chapter Eight 35
Chapter Nine 37
Chapter Ten 40
Chapter Eleven 42
Chapter Twelve 45
Chapter Thirteen 48
Chapter Fourteen 52
Chapter Fifteen 55
Chapter Sixteen 58
Chapter Seventeen 61
Chapter Eighteen 65
Chapter Nineteen 66
Chapter Twenty 71
Chapter Twenty-one 74
Chapter Twenty-two 77
Chapter Twenty-three 80
Chapter Twenty-four 85

Chapter Twenty-five..90
Chapter Twenty-six..94
Chapter Twenty-seven..97
Chapter Twenty-eight..99
Chapter Twenty-nine... 102
Chapter Thirty.. 105
Chapter Thirty-one.. 108
Chapter Thirty-two...110
Chapter Thirty-three...114
Chapter Thirty-four...118
Chapter Thirty-five.. 122
Chapter Thirty-six... 125
Chapter Thirty-seven... 129
Chapter Thirty-eight.. 134
Chapter Thirty-nine... 140
Chapter Forty.. 146
Chapter Forty-one... 150
Chapter Forty-two... 154
Chapter Forty-three...159
Chapter Forty-four... 162
Chapter Forty-five... 167
Chapter Forty-six... 170
Chapter Forty-seven.. 173
Chapter Forty-eight... 176
Chapter Forty-nine.. 181
Chapter Fifty.. 183
Chapter Fifty-one... 186
Chapter Fifty-two 191
Chapter Fifty-three.. 196

CHAPTER ONE

L.T. Stafford was already staring at the clock radio when the alarm sounded. Ruby let out a muffled moan and rolled onto her side to read the time.

"Jesus, 4:30 already." She glanced at L.T. "Don't tell me you didn't sleep again," she said.

"What man could possibly sleep lying next to such a bare-naked beauty?" he said.

"Flatterer." She switched on the lamp on the nightstand. "That'll get you anything your body desires."

"Now?"

"Of course, not now. The diner doesn't open itself." She sat up and let the sheet fall in her lap exposing her bare breasts, soft and supple in the dim glow from the lamp. "You coming for breakfast?"

He reached over to cup her left breast and gently squeezed. "Not if you don't stop teasing me."

"We're best friends, L.T. Best friends always tease each other."

They both stopped short of the 'L' word even though they had been seeing each other since L.T.'s divorce ten years earlier.

"Breakfast sounds good. After my ride." He squeezed her breast again. "I'll have two fried eggs just like these."

Ruby peered down at her chest. "You think I'm flat." She swatted his hand. "I'm not flat."

"Best friends tease."

1

L.T. shaved, showered and dressed in uniform. He headed into the kitchen and poured a steaming cup of the coffee Ruby had brewed, gulping it down as though it were cold water. Donning his black leather riding jacket with the word 'CHIEF' printed on the back he gave her a quick kiss and a squeeze.

"Be careful," she said.

"You know me; I'm a cop. Cops are always careful."

He kissed her again then made his way into the garage. The motion detector triggered the light on the ceiling. The black and gold Harley-Davidson Road King Police Special gleamed in the glow. The bike was mostly original factory equipped except for some chrome 'Live to Ride' accessories and a set of custom exhaust pipes that produced a mellow rumble just a decibel or two above the noise bylaw but nobody complained. The people of White Falls, Ohio seemed happy to have L.T. as Police Chief. He was too well liked for them to ever ruffle his feathers.

Popular or not L.T. was not about to upset his neighbors by firing up a roaring motorcycle in the garage of his townhouse at 5:30 in the morning. He trundled the bike quietly down the sloping driveway and on up the street a few yards. Straddling the machine he buckled his helmet, zipped his jacket, tugged on riding gloves and hit the starter. The engine fired instantly, its classic twin cylinder throb split the silence on a chilly morning in early May. He slipped the shifter into first and as always, rode north on River Road following the winding Sandusky out of town toward Lake Erie. Where the river met the lake, he swung a right turn onto State Route 2 and rode east for fourteen miles following the lakeshore. Leaning into another right turn put him onto US 6 heading southwest for 23 miles. A final right onto US 20 and in two minutes he rode back into White Falls, pulling up in front of Ruby's Diner.

Carla Sears rolled her rented pickup truck slowly past the diner as L.T. dismounted and stepped inside.

"Same routine every morning," she said to herself. "Tomorrow, L.T. Stafford." She patted the stolen Walther PPK in her jacket pocket. "Tomorrow we even the score." She sped up, driving west on Route 20 toward the truck stop just south of Toledo at Stony Ridge.

The diner was packed, as usual. L.T. greeted familiar faces all around then slid into a booth occupied by Officers Joe Patterson and Emerson Weaver, the latter L.T.'s second in command.

"Morning, Chief," said Weaver.

Priscilla Mackie set a steaming cup of coffee in front of L.T. "Breakfast will be ready shortly, Chief," she said.

"Can I ask you a question, Chief?" said Patterson.

L.T. nodded, sipping his coffee.

"How come you make all of us wear body armor and you don't wear any?"

"I just forgot, that's all."

Weaver chuckled.

"You forget every day?" said Patterson.

"It's hell getting old," said L.T. "You get so forgetful."

"You're not old."

"I'm 54; I wouldn't exactly call that young. Besides, it's White Falls; it's a small town. You think some jaywalker is going to draw on me?"

"But Chief-."

"Let it go, Joe," said Weaver.

Priscilla brought L.T.'s breakfast and a fresh pot of coffee. L.T. thanked her, digging into his hash and eggs, perfectly sunny side up.

After breakfast L.T. rode over to the Police Station, the morning sun rising behind him. He parked the Harley in its designated spot behind the single-story building, the basement of which was occupied by the six-person police force. Ground level housed the town hall. As L.T. entered the rear door and went down the stairs, day dispatcher/IT person Annie Maguire called out to him, "Captain Connor called you, Chief."

"Thank you, Annie. Good morning." L.T. went to his office and sat down at his desk. He speed dialed the Ohio State Highway Patrol in Toledo. When an officer answered he gave his name and asked for Captain Connor.

"Morning, L.T. How was your ride this beautiful morning?"

"Always good to get my goatee in the breeze, Chet. What's up?"

"Patty and I are planning to have dinner at Nicolo's on the lake Saturday. "We'd love for you and Ruby to join us."

"Sweet," said L.T. "Meet you there."

"Great. Cocktails at 7:00." Chet hung up.

CHAPTER TWO

The next morning L.T. rose early and made coffee for one. Ruby's Maltese puppy Lola had come home from Doc Fuller's the night before following surgery to spay her. Ruby thought it best to keep her at home for the night. L.T. started out on his morning ride. A couple miles out of town on River Road he pulled up behind a pickup truck parked on the shoulder with its emergency lights flashing. He flipped on the red and blue lights, set the bike on its side stand and got off. A young woman exited the truck, left the driver's door open and met him between the vehicles.

"What's the trouble, miss?"

"Are you Chief Stafford?"

L.T. nodded. "Do I know you?" he said.

Carla shook her head. "No, I just heard about how you're a hero for bagging the Iceman Killer. I don't know what's wrong. Something went clunk under here." She pointed to the back end of the truck. "I pulled over to check it but I forgot my flashlight."

L.T. unzipped his jacket and pulled a light from his belt. He knelt to look under the truck. "Don't see anything," he said. "Maybe you just ran over something."

As he stood, she fired. "You killed my brother," she growled. "Now it's your turn to die."

She pulled the trigger again but it jammed; nothing happened. L.T. struggled to reach for his sidearm. Carla ran and jumped into the truck and sped away.

5

L.T., bleeding from a chest wound, fell to the ground, crawled to the side of his bike and reached up for the radio mike.

"Officer…down. River Road…north of 20."

"Chief, is that you?" night dispatcher Ezra Evans called.

No response. L.T. collapsed unconscious.

"L.T.," Evans called, "Come in, Chief."

Again, no response. Evans had already speed dialed the second in command.

"Weaver."

"Lieutenant, something's happened to the Chief. He called in 'Officer down, River Road north of 20', then nothing. Must have had a wreck or something. I couldn't raise him after that single transmission."

"Keep trying. Maybe someone will happen along and answer back. I'm on my way to the scene. Send an ambulance and Fire Rescue."

"Ten-four."

Lieutenant Weaver pulled up right behind the paramedics. He threw open the door of the squad car and sprinted over to L.T.'s motorcycle. Paramedics were checking vital signs.

"What happened?" said Weaver. "Was it a crash? A hit and run?"

"Jesus, no," said a paramedic. "He's been shot."

"What the hell?"

"Looks like a single entrance wound. But he's lost a lot of blood. We're going to need a Medevac."

"I'll call it in," said the second paramedic.

The wail of another siren approached and in a minute a fire truck pulled up. Firemen in full gear poured out and were met by Weaver.

"What have we got, Lieutenant?" asked a fireman.

"It's not a wreck," he said. "L.T.'s been shot."

"No. The Chief's been shot?"

6

"Guess we're not going to need you after all. We've got a chopper coming."

"If it's okay with you we'll stick around. The extra lights will be hard to miss when the chopper pilot is looking for the scene."

"Thanks, guys."

Weaver walked back to L.T.'s side. "How's he doing?" he said.

"Not good, Lieutenant. He's lost so much blood. We've got an IV going but he really needs to get to the hospital and fast. I don't know if he's going to make it. It doesn't look good."

"He's got to make it."

Fifteen minutes later the Medevac touched down in a field next to River Road.

Carla raced north on River Road all the way to State Route 2. She made a left and drove slowly up the Thomas Edison Bridge. Near the top she ran the passenger window down and flung the jammed gun off the bridge and into the mouth of the river. Then she hauled ass west to I-280 and took the southbound on ramp to Stony Ridge. By the time she reached the truck stop it was daylight. She parked the pickup outside the restaurant and trotted out to the back row of eighteen-wheelers where her truck was parked.

She hopped up into the cab of her W900 Kenworth, its bright yellow finish sparkling under the morning sun. When she hit the starter the engine fired immediately, the truck rocking at first, then the Caterpillar diesel settled into a gentle idle.

Carla took out her cell phone and called the rental company, told them to fetch their pickup from the truck stop. She scratched a few lines in her logbook then headed for Detroit, the gleaming stainless steel refrigerated trailer tucking in neatly behind the tractor.

Priscilla leaned into the order window and called out to Ruby. "L.T.'s late for breakfast, Rube."

"I know. He's not answering his cell phone. I'm kind of worried."

Priscilla shrugged. "Maybe he got a police call and is tied up."

"Yeah, that's probably it."

Just then the phone rang. "That must be him," said Ruby. She picked it up. "L.T.?" she said.

"No, Ruby. It's Weaver."

"Emerson, I've been trying to reach L.T. Do you know where he is?"

"Ruby, there's been a shooting. L.T.'s been wounded. I'm afraid it's bad."

"Oh my God. Where is he?"

"On his way to College Hospital in Toledo. A chopper picked him up."

"Is he gonna be, okay? Tell me he's gonna be okay."

"I wish I could, Rube."

"Shit. I've got to get to the hospital."

"I'll pick you up in five minutes."

She hung up.

"What is it?" said Priscilla.

Ruby stared at her a moment. "L.T.'s been shot. Emerson says it's bad. I've got to get to the hospital."

"I'll call in Lottie May to run the kitchen. You go on and don't worry about us."

"Emerson's picking me up." She fought back tears. "I should have told him to come up the back way, through the alley so I could sneak out the kitchen door."

Priscilla shook her head. "Just go, Rube and don't worry about it. I'll let the customers know what's going on. They're all friends of L.T.; they have a right to know."

Ruby nodded. A police car pulled up out front, lights flashing. Ruby burst through the swinging doors from the kitchen and ran to the exit. Emerson Weaver saw her coming and remained behind

8

the wheel. He leaned over and swung the passenger door open. Ruby slid onto the seat and slammed the door.

"Hold on," said Weaver. He flipped a switch and the siren screamed. The tires squealed as the car made a skidding U-turn and shot westward on US 20. Weaver reached for the radio mike and called headquarters.

"Dispatch, go ahead Lieutenant," said Evans.

"Sergeant, call OSHP and inform them that the Chief has been wounded. Make sure they contact Captain Connor and tell him that I will meet him at College Hospital."

"Ten-four. Lieutenant, how bad is it?"

"It's bad. Tell Captain Connor we've got a crime scene we'd like his people to look at."

"Ten-four."

CHAPTER THREE

Weaver and Ruby made it to the hospital in just under 40 minutes. Weaver parked near the emergency entrance. He and Ruby raced inside and went directly to the emergency registration desk. Weaver hadn't had time to don his uniform, hence he was in street clothes and had to show his badge to the clerk.

"I'm Lieutenant Weaver," he said. "We've got a wounded officer just brought in."

"That would be Chief Stafford?" said the clerk.

Ruby nodded. "Where is he?" she said.

"He was taken directly to surgery. There's a waiting room there." She directed them.

They took seats in the waiting area but Ruby immediately popped up and began pacing around the waiting room like a rat in a treadmill, not caring that she wasn't going anywhere, just moving continuously, her arms folded across her chest.

Weaver's cell phone rang.

"Weaver."

"It's Chet Connor. What can you tell me?"

"I'm at the hospital, Captain; Ruby's with me. L.T.'s in surgery, that's all we know. He took one in the chest and paramedics said it was bad. He's in the hands of God and good surgeons now."

"I'll get there as soon as I can," said Connor. He hung up.

"Who the hell would want to shoot L.T.?" said Ruby. "The whole town, no, the whole county, love him for what he's done for them."

Weaver stared at her. "I don't know. But I'll guarantee you something: we'll get him."

"I don't care about that. I just want him to live."

The hours passed too slowly for Ruby and Weaver. Captain Chet Connor strode into the waiting area at 10:30. He was dressed in uniform and went directly to Ruby, who stood and hugged him tightly. Her tears began to flow.

"Sorry, Ruby," he said.

"Oh, Chet. I just can't believe it. Who would want to do this?"

"I don't know, Rube. You wear a badge long enough you encounter psychos that live to see you dead. We'll get him. That I promise you." Chet led her to a chair and she sat.

He looked at Weaver. "Were you first on scene?"

Weaver nodded. "Right behind the paramedics," he said.

"Tell me what you saw."

"Chief's bike was parked on the shoulder, lights flashing. He was on the ground beside it. No damage to the bike."

"No sign of anyone or any other vehicle?"

"No sir."

"So, it was either a premeditated ambush or a random traffic stop gone bad."

"Looks that way. My money's on ambush."

"My team is working the scene. Hopefully they'll come up with a lead. Has he received any death threats lately?"

"None that I'm aware of."

"Well, somebody had it in for him."

"Maybe Orville Hennessey and Randy Pruitt."

Chet nodded. "That's a good place to start. He put them away for a long time when he cleaned up the town."

"They had some pretty unsavory business contacts from Youngstown," said Weaver.

Chet went to the nearest nurse and inquired but she said they wouldn't know anything until after the surgery. Several hours later a doctor emerged from behind swinging doors and went straight toward the uniformed officer.

'I'm Dr. Peters. Are you here about the gentleman with the gunshot wound to the chest?"

"I am. He's a police officer. A good one."

"I understand. He's stable now. Looks like he'll pull through. We had a close call, though. The projectile entered through the right side of the chest, about here." He touched Chet on the chest just below the shoulder. "It rendered extensive damage to muscle tissue, two ribs, various blood vessels, and the right lung. In fact, he almost bled to death. Had penetration occurred on the left there'd be nothing left of his heart. As it is, a little rest and some physiotherapy, he'll be okay. He's a lucky man."

"Any chance I can take a statement from him?"

"Tomorrow," the doctor said as he walked back toward the operating theater.

"Thanks, doctor. Take good care of him." Chet nodded at Ruby and smiled. He walked over to her. "He's okay. He's going to be okay."

Ruby stood and embraced him.

"Thank God," said Weaver. "Thank God in Heaven."

Chapter Four

Carla took exit 47 off I-75 in Detroit. She made a right onto Clark Avenue then swung a left onto Fort Street and followed it past the Bridge to Canada to Rosa Parks Boulevard. Another right turn and Rosa Parks ended when it curved left onto West Jefferson. Carla pulled up in front of a cross-dock produce warehouse and got out to open the trailer doors. Her hands were still shaking as she tugged on the latches, the effects of the adrenaline rush having not yet worn off.

"I need food," she said to herself. "That'll settle me down. Get something after I get loaded."

She backed the rig toward an empty door and gently bumped the loading dock. The shipper met her as she exited the truck.

"Your shipment is ready," he said. "We'll get to loading it right away."

"Thanks. What is it?"

"Hothouse English seedless cucumbers, fresh from Canada."

"Good, they're easy to haul. How many drops?"

"Just one, a straight load to a grocery distributor in Lakeland, Florida."

"Perfect. Less than two hours from my home town."

"Set your reefer at 52 degrees."

Carla nodded and fired up the refrigeration unit, then followed him into the warehouse to watch the loading. In an hour she was southbound on I-75, stopping only to wolf down eggs and grits at the Detroiter Truck Stop, then back on the big road with the hammer down. Surprisingly the breakfast failed to stop the quivering in her stomach and her hands. The radio news carried the report of the shooting of the White Falls police chief and that he was flown to College Hospital in Toledo but gave no word of his condition. It also mentioned that Ohio State Highway Patrol was investigating the shooting but had identified no suspect in the case.

"I hope the son of a bitch is dead," Carla said. She spat out the open window and looked over at the stainless-steel cup engraved with her brother's name in the co-driver's cup holder. "I got him for you, Marlin. Let's hope he's gone for good." As her thoughts began to drift her body motions became mechanical, as though she were on autopilot. The clutch, the brake, the accelerator, the gear stick, the steering wheel all moved repeatedly with perfect timing that comes from a dozen years and a million-plus miles of routines practiced with more diligence than any world-class symphonic musician or Olympic athlete. Her body now relied on those years of practicing, taking care of the motions as if under a hypnotic trance while her mind tripped back to the morning after her brother's death.

That morning she had been running on pure adrenaline since hearing news of the wreck. Throughout the night radio news reports and CB gossip had woven the tale of how a cop from Ohio and a trucker had chased her brother until he crashed his rig against a bridge and died in the process. Everyone had been calling the cop a hero for nailing the 'Iceman Killer'. It had driven her to push hard all night. She was offloaded and rolling just north of Lexington, Kentucky on I-75 that morning when fatigue began to wash over her causing her arms to go limp as a wet dishrag, along with the rest of her body. Whenever she became conscious of it happening, she knew it was time to get off the road or pile up against an overpass herself. Shaking her head in hopes of staying awake, her concentration wandered causing her to lose speed, as the return spring on the accelerator grew stronger under foot. Then a shiny red tractor-trailer had surged past her door. Instinctively her right hand lifted from the shift lever to clutch the CB microphone from its ceiling mount.

"Okay, driver," she had drawled into the microphone. "You missed me. Bring that large car over."

The right turn signal flashed on the refrigerated trailer. Almost simultaneously it had filled her windshield as it swung to the right to take the lead ahead of her royal blue, longnose Kenworth.

"Thank you, Angel," the driver crooned back at her. "Tell me, what's a movie star like you doing pounding the pavement?"

She was quiet for a moment then decided that playing the game might juice her up again, get her up the road a little farther, and take her mind off other things for a while. "What's a nice girl like me doing in a place like this? Come on, driver, you've gotta have more than that."

"I do," he replied. "In my pants."

"Now we're getting somewhere," Carla said, perking up, sitting a little higher in the air-ride seat. "And if you really must know, *trucking* happens to be what I do best."

"Well, what do you do second-best?" the driver asked.

"Nothing I do," Carla came back, "Is ever second-best."

"Oh, me," the driver sang. "I'm in love again. Third time this week. What's your name, Angel, and will you marry me for a couple days?"

"If I tell you my name," she said, "You won't want to marry me."

He had been pulling away steadily after overtaking and passing her truck but now he eased up on the fuel a bit to match her speed so as not to lose her signal on the radio, or for that matter, let her out of his sight.

"I said I only wanted to marry you temporarily. I done seen how drop-dead gorgeous you are when I passed by your window. Ain't no way something like your name could keep me from wanting to saddle you up, Sugar. So, who are you?"

15

"Unh-uh," she said. "You tell me who you are."

"Road Hog," he bragged. "They call me Road Hog."

"I could tell that about you when you blew my doors off. That's a personal problem, all right. But, really, what's your handle?"

"I reckon that's really it, ma'am. Now, who are you, beautiful?"

"Well, you're right about the drop-dead part. My name's Black Widow."

The radio was silent for a moment, and then Road Hog spoke again. "Black Widow. Isn't that the spider that crawls up on her mate's back and bites him after he's done the deed?"

"I reckon it is," she drawled.

"Damn," he cursed. "Well, would you at least promise to bite me on the front first?"

"All over," Carla cooed, waking up, getting into it now.

"How soon you think we can shuck these duds and get better acquainted, Black Widow?"

"Well, where are you heading?" she called back.

"T-town," he replied.

Shit, she said to herself. "Too bad for you, I'm not going anywhere near Toledo. I'm deadheading over to the Hoosier." Might as well play the game until she had to turn west.

"Aw hell," said Road Hog, and the radio went quiet a moment. Then he asked, "Where do you plan to split off I-75?"

"North of Dayton on I-70."

"Well, that settles it then. We'll just boogie into the Dayton South Truck Stop and get our loads off, come on."

That might just give me the opportunity to show that cop that he really didn't kill the 'Iceman Killer', she thought, *because I'm the real Iceman.*

She agreed and the banter continued as they traveled north. After a couple hours they had taken an exit ramp with Carla following him into the truck stop. They backed into spaces side-by-side in the far reaches of the parking lot. He was in her buddy seat before she had the rig shut down so she manufactured a smile for him. The last thing she had wanted this afternoon was to have some cowboy sweating and breathing hard all over her. But she had to send a message to all those people who thought Marlin was the 'Iceman Killer', especially to the cop who'd killed him.

"Tell me something, Road Hog," she cooed, batting her eyes. "You ever done it in a reefer?"

"Angel, I was born in a reefer; I'll probably die in one."

He reached across the space between the seats which allowed entrance to the sleeper compartment, intending to clamp a bony hand on her denim-covered thigh but she caught his hand with hers, their fingers interlocking. The move afforded Carla a second to scan his features. She was relieved and just a bit intrigued with his hard body and rugged lines.

"Easy, Road Hog. Cut it back a gear," she said with a smile.

"You ain't gonna play hard to get … are you, Angel?"

"Shoot no. But I been running all night. This is one woman who's beginning to smell like a man. You'll appreciate me a whole lot more after a shower. Besides," she said reaching over to stroke his cheek, "You could use a shave."

"That I could, Miss Widow." He reached for the door handle. "Let me get my kit and I'll walk you in."

"Unh-uh. Just meet me in my trailer when you're finished."

"I get it," he nodded. "You're married."

She smiled but didn't reply. The cowboy could believe whatever he wanted.

Road Hog whistled. "Damn, there's just nothing in the world sexier than a cheating wife." He hopped down from her truck.

Carla pretended to be busy with paperwork until she saw the man striding across the parking lot toward the truck stop. As he disappeared behind the next row of trucks, she grabbed a pillow and blanket from the sleeper and headed for the rear of the refrigerated trailer.

CHAPTER FIVE

Nearly an hour later Carla emerged from the truck stop wearing shorts and a tank top, her wet, black hair brushed straight back. Both barn doors hung open wide when she had reached the trailer. Her full, red lips curled into a smile for Road Hog, who sat on the van's threshold smoking a cigarette and swigging a Coors, his long legs and cowboy boots dangling outside.

"Looking damn fine, Widow," he said, handing her a chilled can of beer.

She tossed her travel bag up onto the floor of the trailer, popped the top on the beer and sucked in a mouthful before setting the can next to her bag. She swung one barn door shut, latching it, brought the other one to a half-closed position and then placed a foot on the steel bumper as she reached a hand up, locked it in his and tugged herself neatly into the trailer. They sat sipping beer near the doorway, both silent for a moment. Carla hoped the beer and the semi-darkness of the trailer would loosen her up a bit, make her feel like getting it on. What the hell, he wasn't at all bad looking. It was just that her tank was nearly empty; she was running on fumes after a night and a day behind the wheel. She told herself she was doing it for Marlin. She had to send a clear message to that cop that killed her brother and to everyone else who idolized the son of a bitch. He was not the hero people made him out to be. He had not apprehended the Iceman Killer, as everyone believed. Road Hog would be the not-so-living proof of that. She could do it. In her mind she was already rehearsing it. A chill ran down her spine, causing her to shiver just a bit.

Road Hog noticed her little quiver and slipped an arm around her back, letting his fingers curl over her breast. She turned to look at him just in time to meet his parted lips with hers. He locked onto her, suckling her tongue in deep. As his hands began to move from her breasts to her thighs, she broke it off, pushing him down until he lay on his back. Before he could clamp onto her again, she hopped atop him, ground her crotch against his then stood, picked up her travel bag and headed deep into the shadows of the nose of the reefer. She pulled an eight-foot length of cotton rope from her bag, slipping one end through two D rings high on the bulkhead.

She reached for his arms, gently guiding him around until he was standing with his back against the bulkhead. He watched as she tied one end of the rope around his left wrist, the other end on his right.

"Whew," he said. "You had me worried there for a minute. I thought we were fixin' to finish. Looks to me like you want a heap more lovin'."

He reached out to clutch her buttocks but the rope held his hands at shoulder height. She was in control now and she rode him hard, her ass slamming against him time after time until at last they both exploded. She rested a moment, her hands on her knees to keep her from falling down as the energy drained from her. When her breathing finally returned to normal, she eased forward. Donning her clothes, she picked up her bag and headed for the door.

"You forget something, Widow? Or maybe you plan on keeping me around a spell."

She found her beer and finished it, then said, "You ain't a quitter, are you Road Hog?"

He just grinned. She climbed down from the trailer, latched the door shut behind her and fired up the reefer unit, cranking the temperature down well below freezing.

By noon the next day Carla's blue Kenworth was blowing black smoke from dragging a heavy load as she trucked south just a few minutes out of Indianapolis. She switched the stereo to a local a.m. station, turning up the volume to listen to the midday news. Her hands gripped the controls a bit more tightly as she heard the report.

"...this morning the body of a truck driver from Michigan was discovered naked and frozen in a ditch near Auburn, Indiana. Police have not issued a statement as to the cause of death; however, sources indicate that the case bears a disturbing resemblance to that of the Iceman killing in neighboring Ohio."

That was six months earlier. It was like a nightmare with incredible detail but always while she was awake and driving. Carla shook her head and dragged her thoughts back to the present as the radio reported that Police Chief L.T. Stafford of White Falls, Ohio was in stable condition at College Hospital in Toledo recovering from a gunshot wound to the chest.

"That fucking jammed gun," Carla growled.

Ruby refused to leave the hospital that night so the nurses brought her dinner and placed a chair and footstool next to L.T.'s bed for her. He awakened sometime after midnight and asked for coffee, wanting to know who horse-kicked him in the chest. Ruby took his hand and rang for the nurse who promptly sedated him again.

CHAPTER SIX

Chet Connor showed up the next morning with a small arrangement of flowers. L.T. was sitting up drinking coffee. Ruby stood to hug Chet.

"Some guys'll do anything to get attention," said Chet. He looked at L.T. and said, "How are you feeling?"

"Like someone drove a truck over my chest."

"My guys worked the scene but didn't get much. Tire tracks in the soft shoulder; that's it. Not much to go on but we'll run them anyway."

"Probably a stolen vehicle," said L.T. "If so, tire tracks will be a dead end."

"Why stolen?"

"Because it was a setup; I was targeted."

"No shit. Did you know the guy?"

"No, I didn't and it wasn't a guy."

"A woman?"

L.T. nodded. "A very hot woman."

"Description?"

"Caucasian, blonde hair, about thirty, five-six, one-thirty-five."

"Why would a woman want to kill you?"

"I can answer that," said Ruby.

Chet chuckled.

"She said I killed her brother. I don't remember anything after that."

"Vehicle?" said Chet.

"Green pickup truck. Ford, F150 I think. That's all I've got."

"How long are they keeping you?"

"Be back on my scooter in a day or two."

"You're going nowhere," said Ruby.

"Yesterday I sent a detective down to the state correctional facility in Lima," said Chet. "He interviewed Randy Pruitt and Orville Hennessey but got nothing. They seemed glad to hear you got shot, though."

"I'll bet Randy pissed himself," said L.T.

"Any idea who the shooter was?"

L.T. nodded slowly. "Since she said I killed her brother it makes me think Marlin Sears may have had a sister."

"The Iceman Killer? The guy you nailed?"

"Don't get me started, Chet."

"You don't still think the Iceman is alive."

"I've been lying around thinking about nothing else. If this shooter is Sears' sister, she could be the Iceman Killer."

"How many times are we going to go over this? How's a woman supposed to freeze a man solid?"

"Easy. In a refrigerated truck trailer."

"Oh, yeah. Well, how's she supposed to get the dude into the trailer?"

"How do you think, Chet?" L.T. coughed and winced in pain. "Sex."

"You're saying she promises a guy sex to lure him into her trailer then closes the trailer doors and fires up the reefer?"

"It's a possibility."

"But the stiff in Indiana two days after Sears died was ruled a copycat by FBI."

"But what if it is his sister and what if she does drive a truck? All I'm saying is it's a possibility. We've got nothing else to go on."

Chet shrugged. "We'll look into it. And since your mind is so set on truck drivers and you have friends who drive trucks have a look at this." He handed L.T. a national newspaper folded to an article reading:

Victim Number Four?

New Orleans, LA.

FBI agents are expected to arrive today to examine evidence in the rape and murder of a woman whose body was found last night in the parking lot of a truck stop at Slidell, forty miles to the north. Police have not released the victim's identity. Early reports indicate she was a truck driver.

State Police would not speculate whether the woman was the fourth victim of the Interstate Rapist, though, it is believed the FBI has been called in to make that determination.

In recent months the Interstate Rapist has struck at truck stops in Georgia, Mississippi and Florida. In each case the victim was raped then strangled. DNA tests have linked the three earlier killings to a single attacker. As yet no suspect has been found. All three victims were employed as truck drivers.

Police in surrounding states are urging women who drive trucks to always park in open, lighted areas, report anyone or anything suspicious and use extreme caution.

"I thought maybe you could let your trucker friends know and they could pass it along to watch out for this psycho," said Chet. "CB radios can cover a lot more ground than cops."

"I'll make some calls, have them look out for anyone who looks suspicious."

The problem with an adrenaline rush is that it causes overextension and when it wears off, your body crashes. Carla was still on I-75, now in South Georgia and heading for Lakeland. The Interstate System reaches its slender fingers across the continental United States, corner-to-corner, coast-to-coast. For many its high-speed corridors provide rapid access to cities near and far. But for a few its routes become like strands of a giant spider web with long, sinewy filaments stretched out to trap the unsuspecting. Once lured in, a body seldom is ever freed from its grip, at least not for long. Carla Sears, for one, was always close by the Interstate.

I'll probably die out here, she often thought.

Carla loved and hated the Interstate. Barely twenty when her late brother Marlin instilled in her the thrill of trailer-trucking in an eighteen-wheeler they stole from the dark, far reaches of the big rig parking area at the Wildwood Truck Stop where Florida's Turnpike meets Interstate Route 75, Carla had not since managed to get the Interstate out of *her* system. Nor did she want to. For it was life on the super slab that rescued her from a meaningless existence in rural central Florida. Once her apprenticeship had been served as a team driver under brother Marlin, Carla graduated to a stolen rig of her own and life on the road began in earnest. Over a ten-year span the pair earned a handsome living free of the struggle to make truck payments, unlike so many independent operators. When a new truck was required, they worked at perfecting their acquisition techniques in the darkest regions of truck stop parking lots.

At age thirty-two, Carla could boast of having logged more than a million miles on the Interstate System, though never had she come close to having traversed all of its 42,793 miles. Instead, she found herself generally following a north/south track – with the odd California run thrown in – which made her intimately familiar with a few preferred routes. Over time she acquainted herself with every mile marker, exit number, hill and curve on I-75 from Sault Ste. Marie, Michigan to Miami, Florida. On her good days – when she felt fresh and energized – Carla loved that road. But on her bad days – when fatigue enveloped her and weighed her down as if the load were chained to her back – she just wanted to get herself free from the traffic before it swallowed her whole.

Most often a bad day meant the demons were back. Tired, she could still fight them off. But too tired and they just took over. It always started with another flashback of that night and before long she'd find herself in a full-scale rerun of the events that killed Marlin Sears just six months ago.

On the night he died Carla vowed to find the bastard who had pursued him to his death, ran him until he drove his rig across a spike belt placed in his path by the Florida Highway Patrol. This nobody, this small-town ex-cop, L.T. Stafford from some two-goose town in Ohio called White Falls had been on the trail of the killer of Arnold Perkins, a trucker from New York. He'd pegged Marlin as the killer and dogged him until he broke, crashing his rig into the side of a bridge on I-75. Due to overwhelming evidence uncovered with the death of Marlin Sears, he was deemed a serial killer responsible for the slayings of Perkins in a truck stop at Wildwood, Florida; a computer salesman near Marietta, Georgia; a truck driver from Oklahoma whose frozen corpse was found in a gravel pit near White Falls and labeled the Iceman Killing; and a Maryland State Trooper gunned down in a truck stop outside Baltimore.

Through subsequent news stories Carla learned that this ex-cop L.T. Stafford had been credited with solving all four murders, rescuing victim number five from the killer's tractor-trailer rig, and apprehending the killer, albeit dead. Stafford was later reinstated by the White Falls Police Department and appointed Chief of Police. This small-town hero appeared on television daily for weeks as he made his way from news casts to talk shows. A book was in the works and soon a television movie would glorify his life.

Glorify. Only problem was Marlin Sears did not murder Arnold Perkins, nor was he the Iceman Killer. The cops and the

FBI and even Stafford should have known at least the latter. Two days after Marlin's death another frozen cadaver was found in Indiana. Instead of continuing the hunt for the Iceman Killer, they labeled it a copycat killing and the case remained unsolved. Only one person knew that Marlin Sears had killed only two people. Yes, he murdered a computer salesman from Georgia and a Maryland State Trooper, but not the others. The real Iceman — the real serial killer — was still at large and laying low, making ready to hunt a fourth victim, though not for sport. No. To deliver justice to L.T. Stafford, the killer of Marlin Sears.

Almost immediately after the death of her brother, Carla sold the ranch in Zephyrhills, Florida where she and Marlin had grown up under the thumb of their father, Arlo. Her stolen blue Kenworth and reefer were liquidated quickly also, and she put the cash into a legal hauler: a bright yellow longnose Kenworth and stainless-steel Great Dane refrigerated van. As part of her lifestyle makeover, raven locks gave way under a blonde dye job that proved to be a very close match to her new truck. Marlin would have turned over in his grave. *Never stand out in a crowd. Never bring attention to yourself, or you'll find the sheriff at your door,* he always harped. Well, she was legal now. She wasn't driving a stolen rig anymore so she could damn well do the things she wanted to do. That included honoring her brother's memory by exterminating the bastard that killed him.

But at times Carla had ugly days. Days when she couldn't talk to anyone, couldn't be with anyone and damn sure couldn't tolerate being stuck behind some asshole doing forty miles an hour on a two-lane highway with a legal limit of fifty-five. Beyond tired, wired from the road, and from missing her chance to slay her brother's killer she let herself flashback to that night again, not even trying to fight it. The images of Marlin crashing and burning tensed the muscles between her shoulder blades until she thought they would snap and she spat out the open window.

OVERDRIVE

Running hard for too long she was out of hours. But because home was now within a few hundred miles she pressed on. At Valdosta she had swung the tractor-trailer off the Interstate for a quiet ride down US41 where she was less likely to run into some slick diesel bear that could hassle her over it, or worse, shut her down until she was legal to run another shift. She wanted a bed that was in no way attached to a Caterpillar engine. She wanted to be in that bed alone. And she wanted it now.

But here she was hung up behind some damn deer poacher in an old, red and white Ford pickup with a gun rack in the back window, holding her prisoner in a speed range that refused to let momentum take over. Instead, she worked hard, constantly upshifting, downshifting, clutching and double clutching, arms and legs turning rapidly to jelly. It wasn't that traffic kept her from passing. She was certain that the only other vehicle out there was being driven by some guy named Bubba and he was poking along right in front of her. But with so many hills and curves on the old road she just couldn't get the Cat wound up enough to get around him. She realized her decision to run the skinny road was a bad one, was rapidly wearing down what little energy she had left. That pissed her off even more.

When the road finally straightened south of Jasper, Florida she backed off twenty yards or so and started building speed. The road ahead remained clear. She spat out the window, her right foot slammed the floor, the engine roared and black smoke billowed from the twin chrome stacks. Gradually the rig gathered speed, drawing close to the slow-moving pickup. With the view through the mirrors clear, Carla swung into the oncoming lane and continued to overtake the slower vehicle. Her eyes went to the right mirror. Surprisingly, the other driver seemed to be matching her speed, staying right alongside the trailer tandems. Carla looked quickly at the speedometer, which read fifty and climbing. She grabbed another gear, continuing to accelerate. The pickup went faster, holding its position beside her, keeping her from completing the pass and returning safely to the southbound lane.

Down the road an oncoming car rounded a curve and approached rapidly. Carla reached up and pulled the cord for the air horn to signal the driver beside her that she needed to get over. Twin chrome trumpets bleated a low-pitched blast, their warning moan reverberating off dense groves of pines that lined the road on either flank. Still the driver refused to give an inch. This particular section of US41 offers no shoulder as an escape, only grassy hollows that serve as ditches in the rainy season, a narrow buffer between asphalt and trees. The car drew dangerously close, air horns blared again to no avail. Finally, Carla braced herself, both hands on the wheel, arms rigid, jammed both feet on the air brakes until she managed to get her speed down enough that the Ford shot ahead and just cleared the nose of her Kenworth. At the last second, she swung the rig to the right, almost running off the pavement, the trailer teetering on its air-ride suspension as the car flew past on her left, horn honking.

Carla continued to back off, catching her breath, gathering her thoughts. "You dumb redneck fuck," she shouted at the windshield. "Try that again, I'll flatten your fat ass." The red and white truck opened a gap of about a hundred yards. Gradually the Kenworth's speed increased, then held at forty. The gap began to close between the two.

"Aw, this ain't happening," she said to no one. "Now you're slowing down?" The little truck continued to slow until Carla closed in, then held a steady thirty-five. On the next straight stretch, she tried again to pass. Again, the other driver accelerated to match her speed, refusing to let her pass. This time when the air horns bellowed the driver's pudgy arm came out the window. In the mirror she spotted his extended middle finger. As they approached a hill Carla voluntarily backed off, the vision of another vehicle topping that rise playing over and over in her mind.

On the other side of the hill lay a long, straight stretch of blacktop leading to the Suwannee River Bridge. One more time Carla wound it up, swinging to the left to overtake the pickup. As she drew close the fat, bearded driver leaned his head out the window and blew her a kiss.

"Why you ignorant, redneck fuck," she said, catching another gear. "You'll be kissin' your own ass in a minute." She flattened the accelerator. "And kissin' it goodbye."

The little truck settled in next to the trailer tandems again and matched every move she made. The speed of each vehicle passed through the seventy mile per hour mark. As they neared the bridge Carla checked the mirrors. Nothing in sight except the sunbaked old pickup. She kept the yellow truck's wheels on the left edge of the asphalt until within a few yards of the bridge. With a sudden quick motion, she swung the rig sharply into the right lane as it entered the bridge. The trailer leaned and wagged right like the tail of a dog, slapping the little red and white Ford off the highway. The old pickup climbed the guardrail out of control, smashing headlong into the concrete and steel abutment of the bridge before flipping end over end in a ball of fire into the black waters of the Suwannee River. Flames reached skyward from the murky surface, giving off choking black billows of smoke as the vehicle disappeared on its way to the riverbed. Without slowing down Carla checked the road ahead and behind. There were no other vehicles in sight. No witnesses. And she rolled on.

CHAPTER SEVEN

Roxanne Steel wheeled the yellow Peterbilt into the big rig parking area of the Pensacola Truck Stop, just off Interstate 10 on the Florida panhandle. The Caterpillar diesel clattered as it idled past rows of parking spaces, some with trucks. The huge parking lot held only a third of its capacity on this Tuesday morning, as most drivers took advantage of daylight hours for the business of moving freight, while only those without hours, without energy or without a load rested now. Her eyes glazed, barely open as she leaned over the steering wheel and swung the longnose tractor in a wide arc then straightened out and lined up to a space between an empty flatbed and a load of pine logs. The refrigerated, stainless steel Great Dane trailer followed perfectly. Air brakes hissed as the giant transport eased to a stop without rocking, its engine settling to a prattling idle that gently swayed the cab, making her crave sleep even more.

She pushed her sunglasses up on her forehead, rubbed her gravelly eyes and ran her fingers through her short, blonde locks. The decision to cut her hair had come soon after the death of her husband and partner, Nicholas Steel, murdered by persons unknown while on a run to Toledo. Things hadn't been great between them the last couple of years. They seemed to always be on the road and most often heading in different directions. Working so hard and just managing to stay one step ahead of starvation made it difficult when they did get together to find a reason for romance. Besides, Nick had been getting it elsewhere, she was almost certain of that. Still, she missed the man and would never in her life have wished him dead and gone.

Rocky and her husband Nick had operated a struggling refrigerated trucking business using two eighteen-wheelers from their base in Ann Arbor, Michigan. But when her husband died Rocky decided she needed a change of venue and sold the house and Nick's rig but kept her Pete and Great Dane. Mortgage insurance had paid off their place. With that and Nick's life insurance she could have just hung it up but she lived to see the highway stretching out before her, the sun rising over a different scene each day. She bought a little place outside DeFuniak Springs, Florida to use as a base and was almost home this morning when lack of sleep started getting the best of her. Her body slouched in the high-back air-ride seat. She let herself nod off behind the wheel of the parked rig, knowing that if she settled into the bunk, it would be evening before she would awaken. Instead, a power nap would get her to the house. Her eyes would not stay open and she slipped quickly into sleep.

Twenty minutes later she felt as wide-eyed as if she had slept all night. She climbed down from the rig, stretched her long, denim-covered legs and walked toward the restaurant for a quick pit stop and a coffee to go.

Lyle "Zip" Crowder finished his coffee and sweet potato pie and was about to walk out the front door of the Pensacola truck stop when he had spied the shiny, yellow Peterbilt and Great Dane reefer heading for the parking area. He didn't care much for the color, but everything else about it was sleek and stylish, including the polished disc wheels, bright aluminum fuel tanks and chrome everything. He had never driven a large car before, but always dreamed of owning one someday. This one turned his crank. It was sweeter than anything he'd ever seen at the Crowder Brothers Truck Salvage Yard and Used Truck Sales, one of the busiest used truck parts shops in Alabama. Zip's uncle Amos was the only

31

original Crowder Brother left and he wasn't involved much in the business any more. Amos' two sons Virgil and Jesse owned and operated the yard after their father cheated Zip's old man out of his share of the business and Zip's inheritance. Zip had long since managed to bury the hatchet in the interest of earning some part-time income making long-distance deliveries for them. A smile curled the corners of his mouth as he watched the pretty woman park the fancy rig next to his load of logs.

Zip thought they ought to turn the salvage business into a chop shop. He and Jamal Wissler, an old high school friend who now lived in Montgomery could cruise truck stops away from the Dothan area and steal to order. They could make a sweet living snatching late model tractors and running them to the chop shop. Clean, easy work that pays cash. He even went so far as to get Jamal to teach him how to break into and steal trucks. But Virgil and Jesse wouldn't buy it. They called him a dumb ass redneck and said he'd just bring the law down on them. So, Zip used his unlawful entry skills to satisfy other, non-monetary urges.

"Oh, yeah. She's a babe, all right," Zip said to himself. He thought she looked like Emma. Or was it, Ellen? There were times he wished he had better recall, so he could savor the experience, relive it. Things just got so hot whenever he got with a woman. He tried to remember the details but everything ran fast forward in a blur. Emma. It was Emma. She had short blonde hair and tits to die for. And die she did. That one happened over on the coast at the truck stop near Brunswick, Georgia two months ago.

That morning he dropped off an engine, a Detroit diesel, at a repair shop in Savannah and decided to run down I-95 awhile, maybe catch US82 west or even check out Jacksonville Beach then scoot home on I-10. Emma had rolled onto the Interstate from US17 at the Richmond Hill on-ramp. As he blew past, he caught sight of her yellow hair and bouncing breasts. Immediately he slowed, wanting another look. Grabbing his crotch, he squeezed and massaged himself as she motored past. There was just something so hot about a beautiful woman handling a massive eighteen-wheeler that made him want to be inside her. But something else made him need to control her, to own her for the rest of her life.

The newspapers were already trying to profile him. *Sadistic*, they said. He liked that. It made him sound powerful. And different. He knew he was different. It thrilled him when they acknowledged it. The courage to be different. *Stalking like a predator*, they said. That made him sound so far above everyone. Cunning and sly, a great hunter. But when they announced that he killed his victims to protect himself, to leave no witnesses they were wrong. Dead wrong. For only he knew that the most magnificent boner a man could ever have, came not from the act of sex but from the act of murder of the ultimate sex object. The murder of a beautiful woman. He knew he would be the last man ever to have sex with this woman. *It's not who starts the game. It's who finishes it.* That thought threw his organ – and his mind – into electrifying spasms that took control of his entire being. It made him almighty. It made him rape each one again after they expired just to finalize the act. To Zip, it had nothing at all to do with witnesses. He followed Emma's rig into the truck stop, watched her park it a few rows back, out of sight from the buildings. When she climbed out of the International Eagle and disappeared behind the next row of trucks Zip donned surgical gloves. Slipping his slim-jim into his shirt he sneaked around behind the row of trucks, creeping up alongside the Eagle. Quietly and quickly, he used the tool to break into her truck. In a moment he crouched behind the curtain that separated the cab from the sleeper compartment.

A short time later when Emma had climbed back into her truck, Zip attacked her immediately. At knifepoint he forced her to undress. Stuffing her panties in her mouth he raped her, strangled her, and raped her again. Finally, he went through her purse, examining her identification and stealing her money. On the way home Zip found himself halfway to Alabama when his erection finally subsided.

D.Michael Day

"Yep. This chick in the Petercar looks a lot like Emma," he said, standing watch to see if she was coming into the restaurant or store. Besides working a bit at the salvage yard, to satisfy his parole officer he also drove an old Louisville Ford hauling the odd load of pine logs up to Runnels Saw Mill near Dothan, Alabama where he grew up and still lived. When no driver emerged from the yellow truck, Zip made his way back to the rusty, orange Louisville and slipped in behind the wheel. He glanced over his shoulder, saw the blonde driver snoozing in the pilot seat of the next truck and decided to just hang out awhile. He slid over onto the passenger seat, sat sideways on it and stretched out his legs. Using his rolled-up jacket as a pillow, he rested his head against the passenger door. After a few minutes he heard a door slam and peered over the dash to see the shapely young woman strolling toward the restaurant.

"Would you just look at that sweet ass," he said to himself, and scrambled down from the Louisville, tugging a pair of surgical gloves from his hip pocket.

CHAPTER EIGHT

On the way back to the truck, Rocky's eyes caught a glimpse of the back of a head in the passenger window of the yellow cab. It was Beau. The ruddy Doberman pinscher had been riding with her about three weeks since their paths crossed late one night at the Port of Miami. Rocky had been parked in line waiting to unload early the next morning and was badly in need of relieving herself but the nearest facility happened to be a biker bar a good half-mile away. The second-last thing she wanted to be doing in the middle of the night in Miami was walking the streets of the port district alone. The very last was entering a biker bar in that neighborhood. But to pull out and head for a truck stop would mean she would lose her place in line and probably have to wait until late the next day to offload. So, she had slipped quietly out of the truck and into the April night and began jogging silently along between the line of trucks and the chain-link fence that enclosed the docks area.

The ribbon of semis stretched into the night. Diesel-powered refrigeration units rattled and hummed a constant din and kept her peering over her shoulder in case someone might be sneaking up from behind. At some point – she wasn't quite sure when or how – she became aware of a presence traveling with her and stole a glance down to see the large, red dog trotting alongside. She reached a hand down to pat his back. He never looked up, never broke stride, just continued at her side. When she slowed to get her breath, the dog slowed with her.

As they neared the next truck in line, the click of a door latch caught their ears over the drone of the reefers and they both pulled up abruptly. The driver's door swung open, the dog sidled toward Rocky, set his shoulder firmly against her leg and bared his teeth in a silent snarl, eyes focused on the truck door. White fangs glared momentarily under the glow of a streetlight and the door quickly slammed shut. Rocky and her bodyguard shuffled slowly past the truck. When they cleared the line and moved out onto the street, she stopped to pat him again.

"Nice work," she said and stroked his head. "Okay, you've got the job."

When they reached the bar, the pair entered together without hesitation and while the noise of men drinking and partying suddenly stopped at the sight, no one made a move or a sound as the pretty young blonde with the mean-ass, fur-covered razor made her way to the ladies room. It was still quiet when they walked back out. When one curious biker followed them out the door the dog wheeled in a flash and bared his teeth in a loud, gritty growl. Startled, the tattooed hulk jumped backward and fell through the door, tumbling over a table to the sound of crashing furniture, breaking glass and raucous laughter.

"Thanks, Beau." Rocky kneeled down and hugged the animal. "I'm going to call you Beau. You're my best beau. Let's go find you something to eat."

CHAPTER NINE

Now at Pensacola, as she reached for the handle of the driver's door Rocky caught the unmistakable low roll of Beau's snarl and it made the short hairs prick up on her nape. It was his hold growl. That meant someone had to be in there with him, and Beau was holding the stranger. She opened the door slowly, letting the dog see her. His guttural threat continued as she hoisted herself into the cab and leaned across the seat to peer into the sleeper at the object of the dog's menacing demeanor. A large man with wavy, sand-colored hair sat perfectly still on the lower berth, beads of sweat clinging to his forehead, his hands resting in his lap.

"Lady," he whispered without moving, without taking his eyes off the animal. "Get this dog out of here."

"How about you getting out of here, mister?"

"I've been trying to for ten damn minutes."

"What are you doing in here?"

"Must have got in the wrong truck by mistake, thought this was mine."

"You shouldn't fuck with me, redneck."

"Yeah? Why's that?"

She looked over at the dog. "He's bad, Beau."

The Doberman barked sharply. The sound made Zip's ears ring and he scrambled backward against the wall of the sleeper. "Okay, okay. Just call him off."

"I don't think so," said Rocky. She looked down at the slim-jim lying on the floor between the seats. "You're a truck thief." She reached for her cell phone in its rest on the dash. "Bet the Florida Highway Patrol would like to have a word with you."

"Aw, come on lady," he was still whispering. "Okay, I'm a thief, but I'm not a truck thief."

"So, what are you stealing from me?"

"Nothing."

She started punching 911 on the phone's keypad.

"Okay, okay," he said. The stranger reached a hand behind his back.

"Watch him, Beau," said Rocky.

The animal jumped down from the seat and moved across the floor to within inches of Zip, growling ever louder. Zip slowly turned sideways, leaned away from the dog and pointed to his hip pocket. "In there," he said. "In my pocket."

Rocky leaned into the sleeper and slid the tips of two fingers into his pocket and retrieved the item.

"Jesus Christ," she wailed. "You fucking pervert." She shook her head. "You stole my panties?"

"I'm sorry lady. I don't know what came over me. I saw you walking into the truck stop and you just looked so good I couldn't help myself. I swear I've never done anything like this before." He looked at the floor. "And I don't think either of us really wants to try to explain this to the FHP. Do you?" He paused but she didn't answer. "Besides, I'd really rather sniff them with you in them." He tried a weak smile.

"Mister, get the fuck out of here and never come back or I'll give Beau the sign and they'll be finding pieces of you a month from now." She grabbed Beau by the collar and pulled him toward her. Zip slipped across the passenger seat and stopped to say something, but Rocky shouted, "Get out, you sick bastard." He snatched up the slim jim and jumped out the passenger door.

The Caterpillar fired up with a roar. Rocky jammed it into gear, released the brakes and felt the cab lurch as she let the clutch up a bit too fast, overcompensating with too much fuel but she needed to get out of there. The left side of the Peterbilt rose as the torque twisted it under Rocky's heavy foot. She was blasting through the gears, still in the parking lot but heading for the Interstate. Black smoke belched from twin chrome stacks, the truck picking up speed, its trailer leaning sharply on air-ride suspension as it swung onto the ramp to I-10 east.

Zip couldn't take his eyes off the bright yellow truck and shiny trailer as it motored onto the big road and began to fade into the distance. "She loves me," he said out loud. He pulled the truck's registration card from his shirt pocket and studied it. "DeFuniak Springs, nice town. The town where my new woman lives." Then from a front pocket of his jeans he pulled the other pair of panties he had stolen from the wardrobe in the sleeper compartment of that yellow truck, held them to his face and inhaled deeply.

CHAPTER TEN

Rocky continued east and was just a half-hour from home when her cell phone rang. She reached over on the dash, punched the button and spoke aloud using the hands-free rig. Her eyes never left the road. "This is Rocky," she said a bit too sharply, still running on adrenaline from the encounter with the panty snatcher.

"Hey, Rocky, it's Boston. Are you okay? You sound a little upset, like you're not exactly glad to hear from me."

"That depends. Did you call to say you want to give me a bonus?"

"I'm afraid not, but I am glad I caught you. I'm in a real jam-."

"Don't start that crap with me, Boston. I'm a short thirty minutes from the house, I haven't had a day off at home in six weeks and the United States Postal Service slows down every time one of your checks makes its way into the system, which ain't often enough. Are you getting what I'm saying?"

"Oh, let me get this straight. Are you saying that you've forgotten that back when you and Nick were struggling the only one who'd give you work was yours truly? Are you also forgetting that when poor Nick passed on it was old Boston who made sure all the bills were paid while you dealt with the loss? Are you saying you're no longer grateful for that?"

"You know something Boston? I met the cockroach from hell this morning. The son of a bitch broke into my truck and I

40

thought that was just the lowest, meanest thing to do but I have to tell you, you're down there crawling with him right this minute."

He chuckled. "Isn't it great that we can count on each other when the wheels are falling off?"

"Just makes me warm and fuzzy all over. Or is it nauseous? Shit. What is it, Boston?"

"How far are you from Fort Pierce?"

"Christ, I'm seven hours off."

"No problem, you go to Wheatley's in Fort Pierce for a load of oranges. They'll hold the doors open until six this evening for you. It's ten now, that gives you an hour with nothing to do. What could be better than that?"

"What the hell's so important about oranges?"

"It's not a hot load or anything like that. But you know Vernon Wheatley's a good customer and when he tells me he needs these oranges off the floor to make room for the next run tomorrow, I have to get them out of there or he finds trucks elsewhere."

"You got any idea how tired I am?"

"Listen, you get this load on and you take your time running it up to Dayton. Hell, deliver it Monday if you like. Then deadhead up to see me; I'll have a check for you. You take a day off; visit family; pick up a load of dry freight Wednesday and you're on your way home."

"You're too good to me," she said sarcastically, but as usual Jimmy Boston from Boston Forwarding of Michigan had already hung up. "Looks like we're still working, Beau." She leaned around to look at the red dog curled up on the floor of the sleeper compartment and then turned back to focus on the road, gripped the large wheel with both hands and depressed the accelerator a little farther.

CHAPTER ELEVEN

Zip had dallied at getting to the saw mill to offload the pine logs so it was late afternoon before he made it back to the salvage yard. He shut down the Louisville in its usual parking spot along the outside of the fence in front of the shop, making it accessible after hours in case he should need to haul a load. Virgil was on the phone at the front counter, taking it from his ear a moment to tell Zip to go out back and help Jesse fire up a Cummins engine he had been rebuilding. Zip found the younger Crowder brother leaning over the inline six-cylinder engine of an old Western Star.

"Goddam piece of shit," he muttered.

"Same to you, Reb," said Zip.

Jesse Crowder turned to see his cousin approaching. Placing a foot atop a steering tire he climbed over the truck's front wheel and out of the engine compartment to stand on the ground, wiping his hands with a greasy rag.

"Trouble?" asked Zip.

"Naw, just slapped her back together. Guess I didn't really get enough oil on the cylinder walls so she can't quite build the compression she needs to fire. I thought the oil pump might get enough on the walls but like the rest of this old heap, it's tired too." He reached into the cab to retrieve an aerosol can from under the seat. Handing it to Zip he said, "Spray some of this starting fluid in the air cleaner while I crank it."

42

Zip held the can up to the inlet of the breather, spraying liberally. Some of the fumes blew back in his face causing him to wince. "Whew. A man could sure get high on this shit in a hurry."

Jesse cranked the engine. It began to shudder and rock and knock loudly as the ether mixture exploded atop the pistons. Zip continued spraying a moment until the engine began to level out a bit, firing on four, then five, then smoothing out as all six cylinders fired diesel fuel.

Zip stared at the aerosol can in his hand. "Good shit," he said to Jesse. "Mind if I keep it?"

Jesse shrugged his shoulders. "We got lots."

"It'll make good mad dog repellant."

"Huh?" said Jesse. "You spray that shit on a dog, as soon as he sniffs a good whiff, he'll be out cold."

"Yeah, that's what I mean."

Jesse shook his head. "Zip," he said, "It's rednecks like you that make Alabama everything folks say it is."

"Ain't it so?" The two men laughed.

Rocky got the oranges loaded just before closing time, making Mr. Wheatley, Jimmy Boston and herself happy. Feeling the fatigue, she left the packinghouse in Fort Pierce via I-95 north and drove ten miles to the truck stop at Vero Beach. It was early enough in the evening that she was able to find a parking spot in the front row. After her experience with the panty pervert, she vowed always to park within sight of the restaurant.

She shut the truck down and switched on the auxiliary air conditioner. Beau slipped down from his perch on the co-driver seat and looked up at her.

"I know, boy," said Rocky. "Time for supper. Me too." She fed and watered him then took him out for a walk. Back in the truck Rocky packed her tote with fresh clothes and headed for the showers. When she was finely scrubbed, she found a seat in the restaurant and ordered chicken fried steak with baked potato and

43

green beans. Halfway through her meal the road caught up with her and she yawned. *Going to be an early night*, she thought, *no alarm clock tonight*. In a few minutes Rocky was back in the truck and dressed in her sleeping clothes. She slipped into the berth. Sleep came quickly.

CHAPTER TWELVE

The next morning Beau awakened Rocky at 8:30. She couldn't believe she had slept twelve hours.

"Thanks, boy," she said. "Guess you're ready for breakfast."

He gave a soft yelp and wagged his bobbed tail. She fed and watered him then took him out for a walk on the grassy area next to the driveway into the truck stop. Rocky watched as a bright yellow longnose Kenworth turned into the entrance and headed for the back row. She caught sight of the CB handle lettered on the left trailer door.

"Black Widow," Rocky said to Beau. "She must have some kind of history."

Beau and Rocky headed back to the Peterbilt. Rocky opened the passenger door and Beau hopped up and in, then Rocky headed into the restaurant for breakfast. To her surprise the booths and tables were all occupied so she took a seat at the counter. A waitress approached with a menu and a coffee pot and poured her a steaming cup.

"Want breakfast, Hon?" the waitress asked.

Rocky nodded. "Eggs sunny side up and corned beef hash."

"Comin' right up."

Rocky spotted the blonde woman that had driven the yellow Kenworth into the parking lot. She sat across from Rocky at the u-shaped counter, smiled and gave a nod.

"You must be Black Widow," said Rocky.

45

"Yes ma-am," said Carla. "And you are?"

"Rocky. How'd you get such a sinister handle?"

"Long story. How about you, Rocky?"

"Short story. Short for Roxanne."

Carla nodded. They chatted through breakfast, then Rocky bid goodbye and left, heading north on I-95.

L.T. dozed lightly until his cell phone next to the bed jolted him awake. Ruby looked at it but said nothing. Without rising L.T. picked it up and said, "L.T."

"You can't be sleeping, eh. It's morning."

"Who sleeps? You know me better than that."

"Oh, I get it. You're in the afterglow. Don't you tell me you're riding Ruby from the diner? She's too young and way too cute for you."

L.T. looked at Ruby. "Doobie says he loves you, Hon'."

"You tell Panama Red I've got a bone to pick with him."

"I heard that," said Doobie. "Tell her I've been waiting a long time for that action."

"I don't think that's exactly what she has in mind."

"I was afraid of that," Doobie said. "How you doing?"

"Not too bad considering I took a bullet in the chest."

"You're shot? No shit?"

"No shit. I'm in hospital in Toledo."

"Are you gonna be okay?"

"Oh yeah, doc says I'll be fine. I just wish they'd pull this damn tube out of my chest so I can get out of here."

"Just relax and stay as long as they'll have you; you've earned it. Say, a friend of yours was asking about you."

It didn't register at first. He tried to think of whom Doobie might run across on the Interstate System that would know to ask the trucker about him. "Ray White? You ran into Ray in Florida?"

"Not the lawyer, no. Another sweet young thing."

"Well, who was it?"

"I'm not really sure, eh. She said her handle was Black Widow. Does that ring a bell?"

"No, not at all. What did she look like?"

"My CB communicator ain't got no video screen, officer."

"You talked to her on the CB? What was she driving?"

"Didn't see her. You know how it is, eh. All these eighteen-wheelers with radios, could've been any one of them. Might have been some chick in a four-wheeler for all I know."

"You're a wealth of information, Doob. What did she say?"

"Asked me wasn't I the one helped that cop catch the Iceman Killer. Asked me if I knew where to find you, eh."

"Did you tell her?"

"I told her they made you Chief of Police. I had to make you look good, eh. She sounded hot. Kind of creepy, but hot."

"What do you mean?"

"I'm not sure, eh. But when she said her handle was Black Widow it kind of made my hair stand up on the back of my neck, just the way she said it, eh. That doesn't sound familiar?"

"No. Sounds creepy. It's even creepier that she recognized your truck."

"Makes you wonder, eh. Take care, Supercop. Catch you later, eh."

"So long Doob."

Rocky was running low on hours as she rolled along in North Georgia so she decided to shut it down at the truck stop at Ringgold just south of the Tennessee state line near Chattanooga. Although she had slept well the night before, the cumulative fatigue of running six weeks with few breaks was catching up on her so she bedded down early and set her alarm for 6:00 a.m.

CHAPTER THIRTEEN

The next morning Rocky went into the truck stop to freshen up and grabbed a coffee to go. She wasn't ready for breakfast. When she got back to the truck Beau was ready for a run so she let him out without the leash. When he returned, he hopped up into the cab ready to roll. Rocky walked through her daily inspection and the pair took off northbound on I-75.

As Rocky and Beau blasted through Kentucky and neared Cincinnati, she placed a call to the produce house where she was to deliver. The receiver was happy to take the oranges early so she mashed the accelerator and the Pete responded, hauling ass northbound toward Dayton. She wanted a free day to try to get a visit with Mr. L.T. Stafford.

Vero Beach seemed a perfect place for Carla to base her new trucking business. In a rented condo near the Atlantic shore, she became all but invisible. Her neighbors were mostly tourists; short-term rentals who came and went without noticing that she was often away for days, or even weeks, at a time. No one in the neighborhood knew what she worked at because her rig was kept at the truck stop next to I-95 when she wasn't on the road. She abandoned the name of the old company, Sears Refrigerated Transport Services, operating the new truck under the name BW Refrigerated Moves, to keep her past buried. At home she kept a low profile, kept to herself. On the road she loved to be noticed, loved to be seen doing a man's job and doing it well.

In the parking lot at the Vero Beach Truck Stop next to I-95 Carla busied herself with readying the gleaming yellow Kenworth and stainless-steel Great Dane for another road trip. The trailer was laden with greens, namely endive and escarole she had taken on late the day before at a packinghouse in South Bay. The fertile muck on the southern shore of Lake Okeechobee coupled with the mild climate in that part of the state proved a perfect combination for the cultivation of leafy green vegetables in late winter and early spring, a time when northerners were growing weary of the lesser quality imports and would welcome the fresher taste of domestic produce.

The diesel refrigeration unit hummed steadily. Carla set a stainless-steel travel mug in each of the side-by-side cup holders on the lower face of the dashboard. One cup was filled with iced tea; the other held the portion of her late brother's ashes that she couldn't bring herself to scatter at the ranch in Zephyrhills before she sold it. She wanted him with her – at least part of him - when she nailed the son of a bitch that killed him. So, every trip Marlin would be traveling with her now as she hunted his killer.

"We'll get him, Fish." She twisted the cup in its holder until she could see the name 'Marlin' etched in the cup's metal surface. "He got away once but we'll get him next time. We'll set a trap for him when he least expects it."

Carla shoved the clutch halfway down, gave the gear stick a wiggle to ensure the transmission was in neutral and then fired the engine. The starter whined, setting the Caterpillar engine to clattering at a rocky idle. After a moment it smoothed a bit so she climbed back down from the yellow longnose Kenworth to begin her walk- around inspection of the truck and trailer, thumping each radial tire with a ball-peen hammer, examining wheel studs and lug nuts for rust, which would indicate a loose fastener, but none was present. She eyed the axle covers for signs of grease leaking but they were clean and shining also.

By the time she returned to the cab to settle into the air-ride seat the compressor had built up sufficient pressure in the air brake system to allow her to get underway. She marked the time in her log, pushed the two valves to release tractor and trailer brakes, and eased up on the clutch. In a moment Carla was working through the gears, gathering speed on the interstate as the KW rumbled north with black smoke blowing from twin chrome stacks. The cup on the right – the one with the name 'Marlin' on it – rattled slightly with a tinny sound. She looked down at it, smiling.

"That's right, Fish. You're on the road again. Back in the saddle." She laughed and mashed the fuel pedal.

The fingers of her left hand curled comfortably around the leather-covered steering wheel; her right hand rested on the gear stick. It was her way of drawing power from the throbbing machine. Every bump in the road, every imperfection in its surface, even the strength and direction of the wind registered in her left side through the steering, while the raw force of the tireless diesel power plant coursed through the transmission, its surging energy measured by connection with her right side. And upward, through her feet and through the motion of the air-ride seat came the feeling of iron muscles flexing and responding at her beck and call. It quickened her breath.

The faster she drove, the more intense the sensations. As she broke through the speed limit the turbocharger whined, its shrill whistle urging her to feed even more fuel and she slammed her foot down on the accelerator pinning it against the floor. The exhilaration heightened until she felt a tingling deep within her as the massive truck's vibrations washed through, around and over her.

But suddenly, as the speedometer needle hit seventy-five, the cup on the right began to quiver and dance, rattling frantically against the other one beside it.

50

OVERDRIVE

"Goddamn you, Fish," Carla cursed. "Goddamn you to hell."

She backed off the accelerator. The truck lost momentum under the weight of the load and the cup stopped rattling and sat perfectly still and silent in its holder. For a moment or two her gaze shifted back and forth between the road and the makeshift burial urn. Carla felt a shiver run down her spine. It was as if he were still there, still ordering her around, still running her life. Still alive. She forced herself to focus on the traffic and the asphalt runway of I-95 stretching into the horizon, trying to put him out of her mind for a while.

CHAPTER FOURTEEN

Rocky delivered the oranges at Dayton and drove north toward Toledo on I-75. When she reached US20 south of Toledo she headed east to Stony Ridge and parked at the truck stop for the night. In the morning she fed and watered and walked Beau then went into the truck stop for breakfast. A half hour later she dropped her trailer and headed east on US20 to White Falls, parking in an abandoned gas station across from White Falls Police Department. In a minute she was inside the Police Station and greeted by Annie Maguire.

"Hi," said Annie. "What can I do for you?"

"I'd like to see L.T. Stafford," said Rocky.

Annie looked her up and down, then said, "I'm sorry, Chief Stafford is out of the office indefinitely."

"What?" said Rocky. "Did he quit?"

"No, miss," said Annie. "Chief Stafford was wounded in the line of duty and is recovering in hospital."

"Oh, I'm so sorry. I had no idea."

"Is it something urgent that you need to see him about? Maybe one of our other officers could help you."

"Oh, no. I really just wanted to talk to Chief Stafford. Nothing urgent."

"What's your name? I can let him know you need to speak with him."

"I'm Roxanne Steel. Rocky. He doesn't know me."

52

OVERDRIVE

"I can give you his card and maybe you can call him in a week or so. Maybe he'll be up and around by then."

"Thank you," said Rocky. She placed the card in her purse.

"Did you park in the back?" asked Annie.

"No, I'm across the street." Rocky pointed.

"I'll see you out." Annie came out from behind her desk and walked Rocky up to the street entrance. Annie looked across the street at the yellow longnose Peterbilt with its clearance lights burning.

"Is that your truck?"

"Yes. I'm just passing through and was hoping to talk with the chief."

"I'll tell him you stopped by."

Rocky thanked her and went back to the truck. In a minute she was westbound toward the truck stop. She placed a call to Jimmy Boston and told him she was ready for a load home. He said he'd call her back when he found something.

Annie called L.T. at the hospital.

"This is L.T."

"Hey, Chief. It's Annie. There was a woman here wanting to speak with you this morning. She said her name was Roxanne Steel and she was driving a semi-truck tractor. Because she matched the description of your shooter, I ran her truck plate. It's registered to Roxanne Steel of DeFuniak Springs, Florida."

"You didn't think to detain her?"

"Sorry, Chief. I really didn't put two and two together until after she was gone. I gave her your card so you may hear from her. And I have her number for you." She gave it to him.

"Good work, Annie. Thanks." He hung up.

Then he called Chet Connor's cell phone.

"Captain Connor."

"Hey, Chet, it's L.T."

"Hey, how are you feeling?"

53

"Much better. They're letting me out of here in a few days."

"That's great news. We were all pretty worried about you."

"They won't let me go back to work for a couple months though. But I need a favor."

"Name it."

"Need a background check on a Roxanne Steel of DeFuniak Springs, Florida."

"Can it wait until Monday?"

"Sure. Thanks." He hung up.

CHAPTER FIFTEEN

When she got back to the truck stop at Stony Ridge, Rocky went directly to her trailer and hooked up. She did her usual pre-trip safety inspection then climbed back into the Peterbilt cab. Her eyes scanned the gauges with the quickness that comes with years of experience. Time to buy fuel. She pushed the valves to charge the brake systems, listened to the tinny sound of the air tanks caused by the pressure changes, slipped the stick into low and eased over to the pumps.

"Good to see you again," the attendant said as she climbed down. "Fill it up?"

"Excuse me?"

"Did you want both tanks filled?"

She nodded, then asked, "What did you say before that?"

"Said good to see you again. Didn't expect to see you again this soon."

"What are you talking about?"

"You were here just the other day. Tuesday, I think." He stuck a hose in each tank and started the pumps.

"Not me, pal."

"Yellow longnose, stainless-steel reefer with a fine-looking blonde lady in the pilot seat. Had to be you."

"Yeah, whatever," Rocky said, and went to powder her nose. By the time she returned he had finished fueling.

"You sure it wasn't you?"

55

"Don't go there."

"Now that you mention it, she sounded like she was from the Deep South. Had that twangy drawl, you know?"

"I know it wasn't me." She climbed in and rolled back to the parking area, found a spot and headed for the restaurant to have coffee. In a booth next to the window, she sat thinking of calling L.T. Stafford. A waitress set a menu and a glass of water in front of her and rattled off the specials. When she left Rocky picked up her cell phone. Time to find out what this guy's all about. She pulled his card from her folio and dialed the number of his cell phone.

"This is L.T."

"Mr. Stafford this is Rocky, Roxanne Steel. You don't know me, but-."

"I feel like I know you," said L.T.

"How's that?"

"I spoke with my duty officer that you saw this morning. She described you as Caucasian, blonde, about 30, five-six, 135 and very attractive. Does that sound like you?"

"I'm not sure about the very attractive part but the rest of it is pretty much right on."

"In that case you match the description of the person who ambushed and shot me. Where were you last week, specifically Tuesday?"

"On my way from El Paso, Texas to Fort Pierce, Florida."

"In that case you won't mind coming to College Hospital in Toledo so that the only eye witness to the crime can clear you. Or were you looking for me so that you could finish the job?"

"Now look, Mr. Stafford-."

"It's Chief Stafford, as in Chief of Police."

"Hey, don't give me attitude; I get enough of that on the road and I've had it up to here. So, stop wasting my time and harass someone else." Rocky hung up.

A few minutes later Boston called.

"This is Rocky."

"Hey, Rock, it's Boston. Where are you?"

"Toledo. Can you get me the hell out of the Buckeye?"

"Oh, yeah. Hop over to Napoleon and pick up a load of hothouse peppers going to a grocery distribution center just off I-10 west of Jacksonville." He gave her the address of the pickup. "When you offload you scoot across I-10 to the house, take a well-deserved few days off."

"You just saved my life," said Rocky.

Boston hung up.

Rocky fired up the Pete and headed for Napoleon.

Chapter Sixteen

Saturday morning Zip pulled his black van onto the grassy shoulder of SR83 just outside DeFuniak Springs, Florida and across the road from number 17229. A modest but clean brick bungalow squatted amid the pines with a couple of palm trees decorating the front yard, which was desperately in need of a manicure. A steel-sided shed large enough to park a truck tractor stood at the end of the lane in back. Next to the house sat a four or five-year-old Chevy Blazer and it suddenly occurred to him that she could have a live-in or even be married. He rested awhile looking the place over. It appeared to be all closed up and without activity. Traffic on the road was almost nonexistent with the nearest neighbor's house a good quarter-mile down the road and partly obscured by the pines. A closer look was in order.

He dashed across the asphalt, jogging around the house to the back door. His left arm reached behind to grip the can of starting fluid tucked in his belt while he rapped sharply on the door with his right hand. No barking sounds emanated and no one appeared. After a moment, he stepped back, and planted the sole of a foot squarely against the door just below the knob, then pulled back to hammer-kick the door sharply. Wood splintered as the door crashed open. Zip grinned, nodded and stepped inside.

The modern kitchen housed gleaming stainless-steel appliances against oak cupboards. The tabletop was clear glass with an oak pedestal and chairs. He stopped for a moment to touch the cushioned seat pad on the chair facing the large rear window.

"This is where she sits that fine ass down," he said, beginning to feel a quivering sensation deep within his solar plexus.

Moving through the rest of the house, he tried to take in every detail of the way she lived. When he reached the master bedroom he went straight for the closet.

"No man," he said aloud. "She lives alone except for that damn dog." He grinned, nodding his head.

Tugging open drawers, he searched until he found her underwear. With one hand he lifted each item, feeling its texture, inhaling its scent. Meticulously he placed the tiny garments in exactly the place he had found them. With the other hand he massaged himself, slowly at first, then more vigorously as his loins came alive. The raging fire inside got the best of him until he slipped a single, satin bikini brief into his jeans.

The cell phone ringing in his shirt pocket startled him and he fumbled for the call button.

"Howdy," he said, when he finally got it to his ear.

"Where you at, Lyle?" said his cousin Virgil Crowder.

"Rounding third base and about to ram it home."

"Shit, too," said Virgil.

"Well, what's on your fevered little mind anyhow?"

"We got a rush delivery to Knoxville, when can you take it?"

"What is it?"

"A differential assembly, not the housing and axles, just the pod and gears. You want it loaded on the stake truck?"

"Naw, throw it on the utility trailer; it's not that heavy. I'll pull it behind my van."

"When can you leave?"

"I'm a few hours away."

"Shit, I better send Jesse."

"Knoxville's four hundred miles," said Zip. "When's it got to get there?"

59

"First light."

"Hell, that ain't no big deal. I can make that. You put it on my trailer; I'll leave right after supper."

"I don't know, Zip. This is an important customer. No fucking around, it's got to be there when the sun comes up."

"When have I ever let y'all down?"

"Ask your daddy that one, Crowder." He laughed. "Get your fat ass back here and get to work."

"I'm on it," said Zip. He hung up.

CHAPTER SEVENTEEN

Rocky had the peppers loaded by 1:00 p.m. She caught US6 east out of Napoleon, Ohio and drove it through Bowling Green to I-75 south. Beau rode shotgun in the co-driver seat peering out through the windshield. At supper time they pulled into the truck stop at Georgetown, Kentucky and grabbed some dinner. Beau had his kibble while Rocky worked on a bowl of chili. She could have shut down for the night; she had lots of time to make Jacksonville. But whenever there was a load in the reefer, she felt the need to press on. So, after Beau's run they headed south.

When they got to Knoxville, she was running low on hours and feeling tired. At 10:00 p.m. they pulled into the truck stop just west of the city and looked for a parking spot. There weren't many to choose from at that time of night. She cruised up and down the rows of trucks a while hoping someone would pull out of the front row but no one did. It seemed everyone was in for the night so she settled for a spot in the back row even though it creeped her out but there was nowhere else to go.

She took Beau out on the leash, wanting him near her in the dark. When they got back into the truck Rocky pulled the curtain and dressed for bed. She did not set the alarm; there was plenty of time to make her delivery in Jacksonville.

Zip ran all night and arrived at his delivery point in Knoxville at 8:00 a.m., right on time. In minutes the differential assembly was lifted from his utility trailer and he headed for the truck stop west of the city to get breakfast. He would have taken a nap except the speed he took to stay awake all night was still working. Just for the hell of it he drove up and down the rows of parked trucks until he spotted a familiar looking rig. He slowed and pulled the stolen registration card from his pocket. Sure enough, it was the babe from the Pensacola truck stop. He drove on until he found an empty spot and backed his van and utility trailer into it. Then he watched and waited. He scratched his head repeatedly, the speed making his hair crawl.

Then finally she appeared, strolling past his van like a fashion model. "I'll have you, Roxanne," he said to himself.

When she entered the restaurant, he fetched his slim jim and the can of starting fluid and slunk away in the direction of her truck.

Zip stood on the battery-box step and used the slim-jim to unlock Rocky's truck. The Doberman's black eyes appeared in the window, then its razor-like white teeth, just inches from Zip's face. Its ruddy snout wrinkled up to pull lips over teeth. Zip grinned at the snarling menace on the other side of the glass, pulled the door open slightly and let loose a heavy spray of starting fluid in the dog's face. The animal jumped backward off the seat, faltered as the ether took effect, then fell to the floor.

Beau lay motionless on the carpet. Zip peered in at him for a moment, then slowly and cautiously slipped into the driver's seat. Once convinced the beast lay unconscious, he made his way into the sleeper, crouching behind Rocky's seat.

Right away Rocky noticed the sweet smell of ether as she climbed into the cab, recognized the heady fumes of the common, cold weather starting aid. At the same time, she became immediately aware that Beau was not in his usual spot sitting sentry in the buddy seat and did not come out of the sleeper to greet her.

"Beau?" she called out. When she didn't hear or see him, she started into the sleeper. Her foot bumped the dog's limp form on the floor between the seats. Kneeling down, she called to him again. Strong hands suddenly clamped about her upper arms, dragging her with great force into the sleeper. Her skull rammed the back wall of the cab. Shaking her head, she tried desperately to keep from passing out. She struggled as the vise-like hands flipped her body to lie face up on the berth.

Her attacker stood over her now, clutching both her wrists in one of his iron fists. His other hand clawed at the waistband of her jeans. The button and zipper gave way easily under brute muscle. She caught a glimpse of his tanned face and sandy hair, recognized him instantly as the creep that had broken in and tried to steal her panties just days before. She clenched her teeth, trying to resist, trying to free her hands but he was just too much for her. Rocky gasped, sucked in a breath as her jeans came down, then screamed so long and loud that Zip stopped momentarily.

In that instant, Beau managed to raise himself up just enough to clamp his pointed teeth firmly into the meaty part of Zip's right calf. Now Zip let out a scream. He cut loose with a deafening wail and freed Rocky's wrists. Zip turned to see the dog's head attached to his leg, blood already soaking his jeans. He reached down, pulling at the back of the dog's neck but the pain surged through him. He could not free the grip of the dog's killer jaws. Zip sucked air through clenched teeth. He somehow managed to slip his right hand into the top of his leather boot, slid out a bone-handled hunting knife and buried it in the dog's chest. Rocky screamed and cried. Beau began to quiver, his head shaking. In one final act of desperation to save Rocky, he jerked his head backward, tearing loose a chunk of the man's flesh and muscle the size of an orange. Jaws still clamped tightly together the dog collapsed, lying motionless on the truck floor.

Rocky screamed repeatedly. Zip gazed at his leg in disbelief. He clutched his bleeding calf, hopped over the dog onto the passenger seat, finally falling out through the door onto the asphalt. Rocky tugged her jeans up, knelt down to stroke Beau's head calling softly to him now but he showed no response.

She clutched the handle of the knife with both hands and pulled. It slid easily from Beau's lifeless body. Moving up onto the buddy seat still holding the bloody weapon with both hands, she peered out the half-open door at the spot where the man had fallen. He was gone, leaving a trail of blood drops on the asphalt that led back between Rocky's trailer and the dry van next to it. Slowly she crept along following the trail, knife in hand, until it stopped abruptly behind her trailer. She jogged back to her truck and called the Tennessee Highway Patrol, then wrapped the knife in a clean rag and slid it under the mattress of the sleeper berth.

CHAPTER EIGHTEEN

Zip stumbled to his van, falling in behind the wheel, his face contorted from the searing pain. Sitting at an angle with his right leg between the bucket seats, he used his left foot to manipulate the accelerator and brakes, which made his driving awkward and jerky, but he managed to get out of the truck stop and was soon pounding down Highway 11 south. A couple of miles from the truck stop he pulled over, took his belt off and strapped it onto his bleeding leg just below the knee to pinch off the flow. As the belt tightened, he let out a scream with such intensity that it raised up a covey of quail from the brush alongside the road.

After a few moments he crawled slowly into the back, found some rags, somehow managing to tie them around his oozing limb. The leg of his jeans, soaked with blood, still dripped steadily into the carpet. He made his way back into the driver's seat and resumed heading south, driving in his half-turned position, left foot on the gas, left hand holding the belt tight.

Entering Lenoir City he pulled into a drive-through convenience store where he picked up a bag of ice, a bottle of aspirin and a six-pack of beer. On the road again he popped the top on a beer, took a long slug and then washed down a handful of aspirin tablets with another big gulp. He tossed the bag of ice on the passenger seat, let go the belt and swung his mangled right leg up to rest on it. He winced in pain again, then relaxed a bit as the cold began to numb his wound. Flinging the empty beer can out the window, he tugged the belt taut with his right hand, wheeled the van with his left, making for Montgomery, Alabama.

CHAPTER NINETEEN

Rocky made a trip to the rest room to clean up. She stood outside the restaurant to wait for the Highway Patrol. In about twenty minutes a trooper pulled in and cruised the parking lot. She waved him over. Several more state cars arrived. Shortly the truck stop became a crime scene, uniformed investigators searching everywhere, interviewing everyone.

"Are you Ms. Steel?" the first trooper asked, as he stepped out of the car.

She nodded.

"Are you hurt, ma'am? That's a nasty bump on your forehead. Would you like to go to the hospital?"

"No, I'm okay."

"Could you tell me what happened, please?"

Rocky looked around at people coming and going and said, "Can we talk in the car?"

"Sure thing, ma'am." He escorted her to the other the side of the patrol car and opened the door for her. "I'm Trooper Bruce, James Bruce."

"Roxanne Steel," she said, as he climbed in the other side. "When I came out of the restaurant and went back to my truck, I found my dog laid out on the floor. Something was wrong with him. I leaned down to take a look at him and this guy jumps out of the sleeper and rams my head against the wall. Then he's all over me, undressing me. I screamed and my dog woke up and bit

66

him on the leg. So, the son of a bitch took a knife and killed Beau. My dog." Tears streamed quietly down her face.

"Can you tell me where this assault took place, Ms. Steel?"

"In my truck." She pointed toward the back row of the truck parking area. "Back there." Trooper Bruce put the car in gear, driving along the back row until she told him to stop.

"What happened after the man stabbed your dog?"

"He left. He was bleeding pretty badly from the bite on his leg. In fact, part of his leg is still in Beau's mouth."

"Can you show me?"

Rocky nodded, getting out of the car with him. She opened the driver's door for the trooper, then went around and climbed in the other side. Leaning across the driver's seat he studied the bloodstains on the floor and passenger seat and looked at Beau. After a moment he returned to his cruiser then climbed back in the truck with gloves and a plastic bag. It took both hands to pry the dog's jaws apart and retrieve the lump of bloody muscle. He dropped it in the bag and sealed it. Reaching down, he touched the limp dog gently. "Ma'am," he said. "I think your dog's still alive."

"Oh my God," said Rocky. "We've got to get him some help."

"Come on," said the trooper, picking up the wounded canine. "There's an animal emergency center not far from here."

Rocky climbed into the back of the patrol car. The trooper lay Beau across her lap and in seconds was flying out of the truck stop, siren screaming. Minutes later, Beau entered the operating room at the trauma center.

Trooper Bruce made a call to the lead investigator at the truck stop, told him where to find the crime scene then sat with Rocky in the waiting room. He opened his notebook and asked, "Do you know which leg is wounded? On your assailant, I mean."

"Let's see. That would be the right. Yes."

"Ma'am," he said, and paused a moment, then looked her square in the eye and asked, "Were you sexually assaulted? That is, were you raped?"

"No, thank God."

"Did you know the man who attacked you?"

"Yes. I mean, no. I saw him once before at the truck stop near Pensacola, Florida last week. He broke into my truck there, too. But I have no idea who he is."

The trooper looked puzzled. "So, you're saying he broke into your truck twice?"

"That's right."

"In Florida and in Tennessee?"

"Yes, that's what I said."

"And you say you don't know him?"

"Never saw him before last week."

"But you'd recognize him if you saw him again?"

"Oh, yes."

"What happened when he broke into your truck in Florida? Were you assaulted then?"

"No. Beau surprised him. He saved me. The pervert was trying to steal my panties."

"Were there any witnesses to that incident?"

She shook her head.

"Anyone witness the attack today?"

"No."

"Can you give me a description of him, ma'am?"

She shrugged her shoulders. "Six foot, two-sixty, dirty blonde hair to his shoulders, thirty-five or so and now one hell of a limp. He'd never have gotten the best of Beau if he hadn't used starting fluid."

"Ma'am?"

"Starting fluid. It's made from ether. It's a cold weather starting aid for diesel trucks, but the fumes are pretty intense. He must have sprayed it right in Beau's face, the bastard."

An hour later a doctor entered the waiting room, tugging a surgical cap from his head. "Ms. Steel?"

"Yes." Rocky jumped up.

The doctor smiled. "We got lucky. Although a couple of ribs were broken, they proved sufficiently rigid so as to deflect the blade of the weapon just enough to cause the wound to be sub-fatal. He's lost a good deal of blood but he's going to be okay."

Rocky let out a long, slow breath. "Thank you, thank you, Doctor."

He nodded and disappeared through the swinging doors again.

Trooper Bruce studied his notes a moment, then said, "We'll need to return to the scene, ma'am."

They drove back to her truck in silence and climbed inside. Trooper Bruce took another look around then said, "Let's go and talk in my car. Bring your license and registration with you, please."

"Here's my license," she said, retrieving it from her hip pocket where she had it waiting for him. "And a photocopy of my registration I got faxed to me from my insurance company. The original disappeared last week, about the time this asshole was in my truck."

"Does the registration carry the same address as your license?"

"Yes."

"I assume that's your residence, is that correct?"

She nodded.

They climbed down from the cab of the Peterbilt. Trooper Bruce gave the evidence to a technician and they sat down. In a moment, he began to speak. "Ms. Steel, we'll look for this guy. There's a good chance he'll show up at a hospital in the area. If he's the Interstate Rapist we'll know it from the DNA recovered today. But if he's not the Interstate Rapist, I'm not sure this will go well for you."

"What the hell does that mean?"

"Well, ma'am, there were no witnesses. If he's not wanted for other similar crimes what's to stop him from saying the two of you just had a fight, you set your dog on him and he stabbed the dog

69

to save himself from being killed. I've got a piece of his leg here; there'll be no doubt in anyone's mind that your dog attacked him. I mean, you've got a bump on the head but no evidence of sexual assault. If he uses that excuse – and chances are he will – you don't stand a whisper of a chance of seeing him convicted of assault and battery or sexual assault or even cruelty to animals."

"What about breaking and entering?"

"Is there any damage that would indicate a break in?"

"No, he used one of those tools to go down along the window and unlock the door. It didn't do any damage."

"Not much to make a case on, Ma'am."

Rocky crossed her arms and shook her head. "I can't believe this shit. You're not going to do a damn thing, are you?"

"Well, yes, we are. You saw this guy in Florida and Tennessee. There's a chance he may have committed assaults in these and other states. We've got a tissue sample for DNA. We'll send it off to the FBI in the hope it matches up with someone on their Violent Crimes list; we'll also check it against existing cases in the area. We'll get his description out and we'll check hospitals in the area. We will also notify Florida Highway Patrol that he has been seen in the Pensacola area recently."

"That's it, then?"

"Ma'am, I'm sorry about your dog. Would you like a ride back to the emergency center?"

"No," she said, and shut the car door behind her.

"Ms. Steel," he called after her. She turned and leaned down to the open window but said nothing. "If he has your registration, that means he knows where you live. I will alert your local sheriff's department that you may be in danger. But," he paused, then said, "Please be careful."

She climbed back into her truck without a word.

CHAPTER TWENTY

L.T. was sitting up in bed going over his notes from the Arnold Perkins case and the Iceman murder. Officer Patterson had brought him the files from headquarters. It bothered him that Marlin Sears apparently had a girlfriend that he had not checked out. Cell phone in hand he punched the number of Raylene White at the Office of the Public Defender in Dade City, Florida. He'd wanted to call her for months. Ever since they worked together on the Arnold Perkins murder case, having spent a torrid night together in a motel in Wildwood. Ray worked on the defense case for Elvis Wood, the initial suspect.

Then it hit him. Elvis Wood's story. Wood had seen Marlin and his girlfriend dump Perkins' body off the US98 Bridge into the Withlacoochee River in the dark of night. Elvis had been just downriver setting trotlines to fish for freshwater mullet. The body had snagged in his lines and when he realized what he had caught he followed the pair to their ranch in Zephyrhills.

Later he tried to blackmail the girlfriend into making him a business partner in the trucking firm but she turned the tables and pinned the murder on him. So, there was a girlfriend. Marlin wasn't acting alone. How could he have forgotten that? He cursed to himself for having missed it.

"Ray White," she said, with a drawl that could melt butter, not to mention L.T.'s defenses.

"Hello, Ray. It's L.T."

71

"As I live and breathe, L.T. Stafford. You heartbreaker. What, you came across my number in the pocket of an old shirt you thought you threw out? Don't waste that on me, hon', I heard that one before. Oh, forget it. I don't care what your excuse is, I'm just damn glad you called 'cause Sugar, I have missed your sweet lips, among other things. Get your pink and white down here."

"Ah, Ray, there you go making me fall for you all over again. I've thought about you a lot. How are you and why in blazes are you working Sunday? And why did I know you would be?"

"I'm wasting away in this no-man town. But I'll come back to life if you just tell me you're on your way to the Sunshine State. Tell me you are."

"I'm afraid not, Ray. I'm in hospital in Toledo."

"Oh, my Lord, no. What's happened?"

"Took a bullet in the chest."

"Are you okay?"

"I'm healing up nicely."

"Thank the Lord. Good God almighty, L.T. Stafford, if you're not just a magnet for trouble. What happened?"

"I have a hunch it has something to do with the Marlin Sears case. You remember that one?"

"Marlin Sears the truck driver. The Arnold Perkins murder up at Wildwood. Yes, I remember. My client Elvis Wood is eternally grateful to you for saving him from a murder charge."

"Wood had contact with Sears' girlfriend. You know anything about her?"

"I do. Sheriff Branford Henry tracked her down. Turns out it wasn't a girlfriend. Sears had a sister, Carla, also a truck driver."

"Bingo," said L.T. "The woman who shot me said I killed her brother. It must be Carla Sears. Is she still in Zephyrhills?"

"I'm afraid not, Sugar. She sold the ranch shortly after her brother was killed and she moved on to points unknown."

"Branford 'Lead Ass' Henry didn't know enough to detain her?"

"He said there was no evidence against her so he let her go. Brother Marlin's death solved the Perkins murder. You be careful, L.T. Violence seems to be inbred in that family."

"Don't worry, Ray. Careful is one of the prerequisites of being a lawman. Thanks for your help. One of these days when I get time I'll sneak down there and kiss you all over."

"Promise?" said Ray. But he was gone.

CHAPTER TWENTY-ONE

Rocky didn't want to leave Beau at the trauma center but she needed to get out of Knoxville. No telling if that creep was still in the area. He was obviously stalking her. She had an extra day to get to Jacksonville so instead she headed for the house at Defuniak Springs.

It was nearly seven in the evening when Zip pulled up in front of Jamal Wissler's apartment, which sat over an auto parts store on Old Selma Road in Montgomery, Alabama. He leaned on the horn a moment but got no response.

"Jamal!" he shouted through the truck window. "Get your black ass down here."

He reached for his cell phone but couldn't find it. Now, on his third bag of ice the leg felt pretty much numb, though he was so cramped up from driving there wasn't much hope of making it up the stairs. Besides, he wasn't sure he had enough strength left for the climb anyway. His elbow rested on the horn. Finally, a familiar face appeared in the upper window and the horn stopped. Jamal waved for him to come up but Zip just leaned on the horn again, unable to comply.

"Man, what is your problem?" said Jamal, finally opening the passenger door. "What the...? Man, Zip, you are whiter than any white man I ever seen. I swear, you are whiter than a virgin."

"I'm wounded, man," he groaned. "Take me to your grandma, the doctor. I need fixing."

Jamal studied the bloody jeans and the stains on the seat and carpet. "She ain't my grandma; she's my aunt. Zip you need a hospital, man. You been shot? What?"

"Attacked by a dog."

"Let's get you to the hospital."

"No. No hospital. No doctor. No cops. Just your aunt."

"Whatever you say, Zip. But man, she does abortions, not reconstructive surgery."

"Just take me to her," he whispered, and passed out.

Zip lay face down and unconscious on the wooden kitchen table in the last house on Blackberry Street. The table sat in the center of the room; the chairs lined along one wall out of the way. Jamal looked on as his Aunt Minnie Wissler used scissors to cut away the bloody denim around the white man's wounded leg. Her bony fingers moved with surprising strength and agility for such a slight, stooped-over old woman.

"He got any money?" Minnie asked Jamal.

"How much?"

"Two hundred."

Jamal fished Zip's wallet from his hip pocket. A tiny pair of panties came out with it.

"Sure it was a dog bit him?" asked Minnie.

"Looks like one-sixty-five," said Jamal, counting the bills. He folded them and passed them to Minnie.

"Dog did more'n bit him. Dog tried to fuckin' kill him," she said, stuffing the money in her apron. "Run down the pool hall, fetch Uncle Otis. We gonna need hep."

Jamal wheeled, darting out the back door. Minnie opened a bottle of hydrogen peroxide to bathe the wound with a rag. The belt helped to slow the blood enough for her to examine the damage. She painted the leg around the opening with iodine, went to the cupboard and poured herself a half-tumbler of bourbon, gulped it down and waited for the men to return.

"Woman, what is your problem?" Otis Wissler whined as he stumbled through the front door, shuffling toward the kitchen with Jamal at his heels. "Shoot, somebody done finally give Crowder what he been lookin' for. What the hell? That ain't no bullet wound. How they do that? Scatter gun?"

The old woman laughed. "What fool talk." She waved a hand at Zip. "Man's dog bit."

"Dog bit?" Otis scratched his head. "Dog eat, not dog bit. Took a slab o' steak, sho nuff."

Minnie positioned the men facing each other at the sides of the table with Otis holding Zip's leg just above the wound, Jamal holding it just below the damaged area. She threaded a large needle with coarse fishing line and dropped it into her second tumbler of bourbon.

"Now when I tell ya, y'all push that muscle together to close the wound. Keep your fingers out the way or I sews 'em to that white man's leg permanent." She fished the needle and line out of the glass, took a gulp and said, "All right, y'all."

With painstaking attention to detail her bony fingers drove the needle deep into the meat of Zip's calf. One by one she worked to place the first row of stitches just close enough to each other to hold the muscle together. Finishing the first row, she took a gulp of bourbon and started to place a second row much shallower to tie the skin over and completely close the wound.

"When he wakes up, he gonna know pain like never before. Tell him he got to stay off it a few days and keep it dry. And when he starts to use it, take it easy for a spell. He ain't never gonna break dance, but he won't bleed to death, neither."

She counted out fifty dollars from her apron and handed it to Jamal. "Go and give this to Doc Swan. Tell him I need a prescription for antibiotics for infection. And you make sure this white man takes every last pill or he'll get the fever."

Jamal went out the door.

CHAPTER TWENTY-TWO

Rocky pushed it. For Beau. She hated leaving him in Knoxville, but she took comfort in knowing that he was getting the best of care. They hadn't known each other long. Still, there had been a bond from that very first night in Miami. And today, he almost gave it all to save her. She backed the trailer in alongside the shed behind her house and finally shut down the diesel on the longest day since Nick died. Fatigue suddenly enveloped her as though she were standing in a waterfall, no longer able to fight against it to raise herself up under its weight.

"Aw, shit," she muttered. "Beau, I'm so sorry." She sat crying in silence a moment or two. When she finally mustered the strength to head for the house something about it caught her eye, didn't look quite right, though she couldn't really tell why under the dim light that shone from above the shed door. As she neared the house, it became clear to her that the door was ajar. Quickly she made her way back into the Peterbilt, locked the doors and called the Walton County Sheriff's Department.

Forty minutes later a pair of deputies arrived. She flipped on her cab lights, waving to them. The police car rolled directly up to the nose of the truck. As it stopped, two uniformed officers leaped from the car, guns drawn, pointing at her. Rocky froze.

One officer called out, "Step out of the vehicle. Now."

Slowly Rocky opened the door, holding her driver's license in her hand, and climbed down. She held out her ID. The deputy holstered his weapon and examined her license briefly under a flashlight.

"Are you all right, Ma'am?"

She nodded. "I just got home. Been on the road six weeks. I live alone." She pointed. "The door is open. There."

"Wait in your truck, please. We'll check it out."

"About five minutes later they returned with the word that all was clear. One went to use the radio in the patrol car, the other took her to the house.

"It doesn't appear as anything has been disturbed inside, Ma'am. The door and frame are damaged but nothing else is broken inside. You can have a good look through and let us know if anything is missing."

"Sure. I know right where to look."

"Ma'am?"

"Sit down. Please." She pointed to a chair at the kitchen table. Rocky took a seat opposite him and began to relate the events of the day and her two previous encounters with the sandy-haired stranger. The deputy let her tell the entire story before he spoke again.

"Were police called to the Pensacola truck stop?" he asked.

"No. I was so scared and so pissed that as soon as he was out the door, I slammed that truck in gear and floored it. I was on my way home that day when I got a call to go straight to Fort Pierce to load for Dayton, Ohio. But I'm sure this didn't happen until after that day because that's when my truck registration card disappeared."

"And it has this address on it," he mused.

Rocky nodded.

"Try not to disturb things too much. We'll get an evidence unit out here first thing in the morning to check for fingerprints and trace evidence." "You won't find any prints. This guy wears gloves. The kind a doctor wears. Latex."

78

The deputy nodded and thought a moment. "I reckon that could mean he's an experienced criminal, Ms. Steel. There's a good chance some other piece of evidence may eventually lead to his capture. Our team will look for things like hair, fibers, shoe prints, tire tracks, and the like."

"Well, I'm afraid I can't be here in the morning. I've got to be in Jacksonville. I only stopped here tonight to get a shower and a few hours rest out of the truck. Need to do some laundry, too, if I have time."

"Ms. Steel, you look mighty tired. Would you let us help you secure the place until you can have repairs made?"

Too tired to argue, she nodded. The officers then helped rig a temporary lock for the back door by jamming a length of two-by-four under the doorknob and wedging it against the opposite wall where it meets the floor.

As the deputies went out the front door, one turned and said, "Try to get some rest, Ma'am. Call us if you need us."

Rocky thanked them, though instead of resting she prepared a bucket of hot soapy water and scrub brush and went back out to clean the blood from her truck. She leaned across the driver seat and reached down with the brush and worked it back and forth. Moving into the sleeper, she spotted something under the berth and went in to retrieve it. Her jaw dropped. In her hand she held the identity of her attacker. During the scuffle he had lost his cell phone. Rocky knew it would lead her straight to him.

Chapter Twenty-three

Rocky finished offloading in Jacksonville by noon Friday, well ahead of her scheduled four o'clock deadline. She headed west of the city on I-10 a few miles, pulling into the truck stop at the junction of US301 to get a bite to eat and have her truck washed, since she never did get around to it in Knoxville. No need to be in a hurry now. She just wanted to get to the house and see to getting the door repaired, then jump in the Blazer and head for Knoxville to be with Beau. Three parking spaces sat empty in the front row of the parking area. Rocky wheeled the rig neatly between the white lines of the middle one. No more parking near the back row. Her truck would always remain in the open and in plain sight to discourage intruders.

She ran the window down and shut off the engine. The warm breeze and sudden silence brought a wave of fatigue that washed over her, draining the energy from her aching body. Too many miles on it in the last few days; too many long, difficult miles. She wished she had someone to talk to so she could just let it all out before her jagged-edged nerves drove her to paranoia, or worse.

The ringing of her cell phone shook her from the quiet of the moment and her hand went to the button on the hands-free rig. "This is Rocky," she said, her head leaning back against the high-rise seat.

"Ms. Steel, it's Dr. Churchill at the Knoxville Animal Emergency Center."

Rocky sat up straight; her eyes widened. "Yes, Dr. Churchill. How's Beau doing? Is he going to be okay?"

"I'm happy to tell you he's going to be fine. The worst is over now and he's stable with good vital signs. He's a real fighter."

"Oh, thank God. I'm sorry, thank you too, Dr."

"Believe me, it's a pleasure. You're the lady trucker, right?"

"That's right."

"Your friend needs to spend a few days here healing from the surgery and building his strength. But if all goes well, he should be up and around about Thursday. Although, I really don't think he should be jumping in and out of a big truck for a couple weeks. Can you keep him home for a while, let him get his legs back naturally?"

"I am so ready for a vacation. This week will be a perfect time to start."

"Fine. I'll call in a couple days to let you know when you can pick him up. In the meantime, you feel free to call any time for an update on his condition."

"Thanks again, Dr. Churchill." Rocky hung up. Her spirits bubbled back up from the depths and she broke into a smile. It was time to call Jimmy Boston. She punched in his number.

"Boston," Jimmy answered.

"Boston, this is Rocky."

"What is this? Psychic Network? I swear I had the phone in my hand to call you this very minute and here you are ringing to tell me you're ready for another run."

"Wrong. My crystal ball is telling me I'm on vacation for two, no it looks like three weeks."

"Vacation? Sure, after next week. I've got loads I've got to move and no trucks. No vacation this week."

"I seem to have a bad connection, Boston. I'll call you back on a land line in three weeks."

"Rocky, here's how it is. You got your choice. You load in Tampa today for Denver. It's a mixed load, peppers and tomatoes.

Or you load Monday in Fort Pierce, a straight load of grapefruit to Halifax, Nova Scotia. Or, hey, here's one that'll put you on vacation middle of the week. Load tomorrow morning in Montgomery to deliver in Toledo on Monday."

"Load what in Montgomery? What, besides rednecks, comes out of Alabama?"

"Believe it or not it's four hundred bags of red clay going to a brick factory in T-town. Doesn't pay the greatest but you don't have to run the reefer, it stacks nice and low in the trailer so you can fly through the turns and it's all palletized; you don't touch a thing and you're out fast. I'll find you a backhaul and you're on vacation before the weekend."

Rocky hung up without giving him an answer. She was about to head into the restaurant when the unthinkable happened. The other cell phone, the one she found under the berth after her run-in with the pervert, was ringing. Her eyes fixed on it in the tray under the instrument panel. It rang again and then another time. She picked it up, still staring at it, then flipped it open and said, "This is the operator. What area code and number are you calling?"

A voice on the phone spoke the number of the cell phone. Rocky grabbed her pen and clipboard and jotted it down.

"And what party are you trying to reach, sir?"

"Huh? Party? I ain't callin' no party. I'm calling Lyle Crowder."

"I'm sorry, sir. That number is temporarily out of service." She closed the phone and sat very still for at least five minutes. Then, after locking the truck she took her clipboard into the truck stop and headed for the driver's lounge. In a few minutes she was signed onto a computer and used the Internet to find a cell phone reverse directory. The area code was Alabama, that much she knew. Before long she was looking at the address of Lyle Crowder in Dothan, Alabama. And Dothan happened to be on the way to Montgomery. She called Boston back and told him she'd be in Montgomery in the morning.

She wolfed down a sandwich and a cup of coffee in the restaurant and in minutes was blasting west on I-10. She was in the hammer lane near Tallahassee rolling past a line of trucks when she heard the siren, shot a glance toward the left mirror and spotted blue lights flashing. The car crowded the rear of her trailer, running half on the paved shoulder to send her a clear message. She eased off the accelerator and signaled right. The truck beside her backed off to let her in and she swung the rig through the right lane onto the other paved shoulder, gently braking to a stop. The trooper pulled in behind her.

She grabbed the CB mike from its mount on the ceiling and said, "Thank y'all for telling me about the bear."

A driver shot back, "Hell, you had to be running eighty. He came up on us just as quick as you."

There was a tap on her door. Rocky pushed the button to open the window and peered down at the officer. "License, insurance, and registration, please."

"Good afternoon to you too, officer."

"Ma'am," he said. He took the documents from her and walked back to his patrol car. In a few moments he returned and said, "Would you lock your vehicle and step outside, please. I need you to come back to the patrol car."

"Can't you just write me up and let me be on my way?"

"I'm afraid not. You'll have to come with me."

"Aw, for Chrissakes, I was speeding, I admit it. Just give me the ticket."

He tugged her door open. "Step outside, ma'am. Now."

Rocky shut down the diesel and locked the Peterbilt. The trooper escorted her to the car and held the door as she slid onto the back seat. "Fasten your seat belt," he said.

The trooper pulled onto the highway, lights flashing, siren wailing and sped toward Tallahassee.

"What's this all about?"

"I've been ordered to detain you for questioning by the FBI."

D.Michael Day

"What for?"

"I'm not exactly sure, ma'am."

Rocky crossed her arms and stared out the window as they overtook the line of trucks she had been passing a few minutes ago. In a while the police car turned off the interstate and pulled into the parking lot at the Tallahassee Field Office of the FBI. The trooper escorted Rocky inside to the reception area where she was met by Special Agent Carpenter who ushered her into an interview room. A female agent waited there.

"This is Agent Cromwell. She's a sketch artist. She'll interview you."

"What for?"

"I'm sorry, Ms. Steel," said Agent Carpenter. "We've had police all over the country looking for you since we got DNA results back on the evidence collected after your attack in Tennessee Sunday. You're very lucky to be alive."

"You're the first person to feel that way in some time."

"Nevertheless, we now know that your attacker was the Interstate Rapist, a ruthless killer of female truck drivers. And you happen to be the only person alive who can identify him."

Rocky sank into a chair next to Agent Cromwell. Her head spun. She knew the guy's identity, even his address. She could lead them right to him. She should tell them, she knew. But something way down inside just wouldn't let her do it. The man needed to be stopped, all right. But not to park his fat ass in a prison cell at taxpayers' expense and someday face the opportunity of doing this again. She'd give them a description and a good one. Let them post his likeness in every terminal and every truck stop in the nation so that no trucker, no woman anywhere would fall prey to the sick bastard. But that's all she would give them. Because she and Beau would soon be taking the fight back to Mr. Lyle Perverted Crowder of Dothan, Alabama. And one of them would not survive.

84

CHAPTER TWENTY-FOUR

Carla offloaded the greens in Columbus, Ohio and reloaded in the same city. The rig gathered speed under Carla's heavy foot, barreling south in light traffic on US23, pulling forty-five thousand pounds of carrots from a cold storage facility bound for the Port of Miami and a cargo ship to South America.

It was afternoon and she cruised into the rolling hills south of Columbus. Still on US23, the yellow Kenworth began chewing up the hills, black smoke blowing from twin chrome stacks. Somehow speed gave her power, cleared her head, helped her to think. Her eyes scanned the road ahead constantly, automatically in search of anything that looked like a police car. Speeding could only be justifiable when she didn't get caught. The stainless-steel cup began to rattle in its holder sending a sudden shiver through her. Carla glared at it, her eyes shifting between it and the road ahead as it rattled on.

"All right," she shouted. "All right, I fucked up. I only wounded the bastard." The cup continued to rattle incessantly. She reached over and tried swiveling it in its holder to silence it but nothing seemed to work. "Settle down, will you? We'll go to plan B. If we can't go after him and nail him, we'll just have to get him to come to us. First thing we have to do is send him a very clear message so that he knows we're still out here. He'll come looking for us and when he does, we'll set a trap for him." She rounded a curve to

85

the left, the big rig hugging the pavement tightly. The cup finally went silent.

Carla eased off the fuel pedal a bit as the yellow Kenworth, which had been passing everything in the southbound lanes, drew within a hundred yards of a familiar looking trailer. She spotted the trademark poker hand painted on the lower left corner of the trailer's doors. The top card was a jack.

"Well, if it isn't Jack," she said aloud, and mashed the accelerator.

Over the CB she said, "Lookout, Jack. I'm about to blow your doors off."

"Who said that?" the driver shot back. "Who is that in the large car? You sound familiar, but I don't recognize the ride. Sure is yellow."

Carla checked the left mirror and swung the rig into the passing lane to go around the tractor-trailer. As she drew alongside the other rig its driver looked over, smiled and waved. Carla nodded and smiled back. As her trailer cleared his tractor the driver called her on the CB, saying, "Spider Woman is that you? I heard you quit driving trucks when your brother died. Okay, you missed me, movie star. Slide that large car over and let me watch your rear."

The right turn signal flashed on Carla's shiny trailer and the rig swung neatly into the right lane. "Thanks, Jack. My brother didn't just up and die, he was killed. By the way, it's not Spider Woman any more. I've changed my name, got a new identity."

"Well, what is it?"

"Unh-uh. I'm not sure I want you to know, Mr. Jack of All Trades."

"Are you still pissed over me dumping you? And for your information it's now One-eyed Jack. One-eyed Jack in the two-stack Mack with the shack on the back."

"You're a little mixed up mister One-eyed Jack, stab you in the back. I sent you packing back to your wife with your little tail between your legs."

Another voice cut in. "If you south bounders can break up the fight a minute you might hear a report about a bear in the rest area at Jackson shooting your side. And if you're catching US35 toward West Virginia the highway is closed down yonder on the two-lane section. Damn train derailed and left three boxcars blocking the viaduct. You might as well find a place to hang it up and fight all night 'cause the road ain't gonna be open 'til morning."

"Thank you, Northbound. You've got a clean shot to Columbus and mind your own damn business about the fighting. You hear me?" said Carla.

The other driver laughed.

"Tell me, Jack. How's your wife?"

"I reckon she's fine. She's moved to Georgia with her new husband."

Carla broke into shrill, piercing laughter over the radio.

"I didn't think it was that funny," said Jack. "You always had this mean and nasty side to you, Spider.

"Black Widow," she replied.

"Black Widow? Shoot, you're prettier than a speckled pup and there's been times I'd trade my little red wagon for you but I'm not sure I'd like to lie next to a Black Widow. That's that nasty side again, sure enough."

"You haven't seen my nasty side, Jack. And what the hell makes you think I'd let your sorry ass lie next to me?"

"Now you're sounding downright cruel. Can't we just let bygones be bygones and start over? Get to know each other again?"

Carla's lips began to curl into a half smile. *I just might have a need you could satisfy, Jack.* "Maybe," she said.

"Where you makin' for, Black Widow?"

"I'm working my way back to the Bikini State. How about you?"

"Beckley, Wet Vagina. Excuse me, West Virginia. Then I'll be looking for a load home. Seems like I been pounding the pavement a long time without a break. I reckon I'm going to grab a beer and a sandwich down yonder at the Continental Motor Inn just outside Chillicothe. You hungry?"

"Not particularly, but a beer might help settle the fleet of trucks rolling around in my stomach."

"Nice to see I can still get you all bubbly inside."

"It's not you, Jack. It's the flu."

"You ever been to the Continental?"

"Can't say it rings a bell."

"Plenty of truck parking, great food, and cold beer. The rooms ain't bad, too, just in case you're tired or need to lay your head down for some other reason like the road being closed."

"You're going to have to start playing your cards better, Jack. So far, you're still a loser. But the good news is I've got until Wednesday to make Miami."

"Hell, Black Widow, I know you still love me. We might as well get hitched for a couple days and get an early start on the honeymoon."

Her red lips curled into a wicked smile.

Rocky rolled into Dothan shortly after dark. She had wanted to stop off at her house, grab a shower, pack a bag of fresh laundry before heading out again but DeFuniak Springs would have added two hours driving time alone to the trip. Ever since Lyle Crowder's cell phone had gone off, she could think of nothing but getting to Dothan. She found a truck stop on the outskirts and shut down the rig there, went inside and called a taxi, then returned to the truck to wait. Before entering the yellow tractor, she opened the side storage compartment, retrieved a screwdriver from the tool kit and climbed inside. Instead of sitting in the seat she went directly into the sleeper, pulled the hunting knife from under the mattress and slipped it into the inside pocket of her leather bomber jacket, along with the screwdriver.

A horn sounded outside. Rocky peered out through the windshield to see a taxi stopped at the restaurant. She hopped down, locked the doors and sprinted over to the car, giving Lyle Crowder's address as she slid onto the back seat.

"No offense, ma'am, but are you sure you want to go there?"

"What's that supposed to mean?"

"Well, it's just that area is kind of rough. I mean, there's a few white folks living there but not many. And they don't look anything like you."

"What do I look like?"

"I reckon you look like you don't belong there. And that's likely to rile folks on that side of town. They don't take to outsiders."

"Doesn't sound very neighborly."

"I'm just trying to help, ma'am."

"Just drive. I just want to have a look at the place."

He wheeled the cab around and out onto the street, reaching over to pull the flag down. Rocky's heart began to pound at the thought of being this close to that perverted bastard. In ten minutes, they turned into a narrow lane alongside a railroad yard full of rusting box cars that looked as though they hadn't moved in Rocky's lifetime. The cab pulled up in front of a row of weathered, clapboard sided frame houses, all of them very small and long in need of paint.

The driver pointed to the third house and said, "That's it, ma'am. That's the address you're looking for."

Dirty screens made the windows look black. No lights burned inside or out, while the grass seemed overrun with weeds and in need of cutting. No vehicle occupied the driveway. She took a good, long look until a chill crept slowly up her spine. She had come here wanting – determined to – take the screwdriver and pry open a door, find the bastard suffering from his wound and return his knife to him, business end first. But the scene was nothing like what she had expected. It was far creepier. And besides, Beau was going to be okay. She knew that now.

She took a deep breath and said, "I guess you're right. I'm in the wrong neighborhood. Take me back to the truck stop, please."

"Yes, ma'am."

CHAPTER TWENTY-FIVE

Chet Connor arrived the next morning carrying two large cups of coffee from Ruby's Diner. He handed one to L.T. and said, "I found out some interesting things about Roxanne Steel."

L.T. dragged himself up into a sitting position. "Yeah?"

"In a weird way, she's connected to that Iceman Killer case you were involved in last year."

"I knew it."

"You knew?"

"She's his sister, right? Her brother was Marlin Sears, the Iceman Killer."

"Unh-uh, it's weirder than that."

"His girlfriend?"

"Will you shut up and listen a minute?"

"What?"

"I started checking her out in the usual manner. She used to live in Michigan, moved to a small town in the Florida panhandle a few months ago after the death of her husband. But there was something familiar about her name. So, I kept digging. Found out her late husband, Nicholas Steel, was the victim in the copycat case. The Iceman copycat case in Auburn, Indiana."

"The victim? She killed her husband, that's why she calls herself Black Widow."

90

"No, she was in Texas for several days around the time of his death. Her truck was broken down in Austin. She was nowhere near that killing."

"Oh, shit."

"Did you think she was a killer?"

"Oh, it's worse than that. I pretty much accused her of it. I was so convinced she was the killer I accused her of shooting me."

"You're lucky she didn't drive that big truck over your thick head."

"Man, I need to call her. Where's my phone?" He reached for the nightstand.

"You'd better hear the rest of it, first."

"There's more?"

Chet nodded. "FBI is looking for her."

"So, she was up to something."

"No, she wasn't up to something. Will you just shut up? She's had a hell of a week. She was attacked at a truck stop in Tennessee yesterday around noon."

L.T.'s jaw dropped. Chet nodded.

"She needed my help and I ran her off."

"You shit," said Chet. "Now listen, it gets worse. The perp stabbed her dog, nearly killed him but the dog saved her by taking a chunk out of the guy's leg and running him off. So, the Tennessee State Police got a DNA sample. Turns out this bad ass has been stalking her. Broke into her truck two weeks ago in Florida, stole her registration to get her address. When she got home from Tennessee, she found her house had been broken into. Tennessee HP gets the DNA results and passes them along to the FBI. The guy is none other than the Interstate Rapist."

L.T. hung his head. "Man, she must've really needed a friend to be calling me and I do this to her. I've got to get out of here." He rang for the nurse.

"No offense, but you don't look fit to be going anywhere. You look like shit."

91

He sat on the edge of the bed, his feet hanging over. "That's what Ruby said, too."

"Yeah, but she probably had other reasons for saying it."

The nurse entered the room. "Mr. Stafford, what are you doing up? Are you okay?"

He pointed to the intravenous line. "Get this off my arm. I've got to get out of here. A woman's life is in danger."

"I've heard that happens wherever you go," she said. "Now get your ass back in bed, you're not going anywhere."

"Look, you can't keep me here. I'm telling you; a woman is in grave danger. I've got to help her."

"L.T.," said Chet. "We've got people watching for her. We've checked with her broker. We know she loaded in Montgomery, Alabama this morning, bound for Toledo. We'll find her when she makes it up here. You need rest. Leave it to us."

"But I owe her big time."

"Well, it won't be the first time - or the last – that you've been in that situation."

The nurse shoved a thermometer under his arm and told him to sit still, shut up and forget about going anywhere. L.T. scowled at her, but gave her no more trouble.

"Guess I'd better get back to work," said Chet. "You appear to be in good hands."

"Hold on. Something doesn't quite fit. Rocky drives a yellow truck with a stainless-steel refrigerated trailer. Doobie said a sinister sounding woman of similar description has been asking about me, looking for me. What do you make of that?"

Chet shrugged his shoulders. "Truckers exaggerate. Did he define sinister?"

"Just said she sounded kind of creepy. Do me one more favor. See what you can find out about a truck driver named Carla Sears."

"Wife of the Iceman?"

"Sister. Doobie says she calls herself Black Widow."

Chet nodded. "I'll get on it. You stay put." He walked out. The nurse followed. L.T. found his cell phone and punched up Rocky's number.

"This is Rocky."

"Rocky, it's L.T. I -." She hung up.

CHAPTER TWENTY-SIX

Zip awakened with his head in a vise and someone cranking the handle tighter and tighter. At least that's what it felt like. He lay motionless, unable to move a muscle, staring up at the single, bare bulb burning intensely, penetrating his gravelly eyes. After several minutes he managed to drag his right arm up to shield his eyes, though he was immediately sorry for the move seemed to enliven the rest of his body and he became suddenly and painfully aware that his right leg was on fire with a hurt that ravaged him to the very core.

"Ain't no surprise," he called out to no one, his eyes still covered. "Pa always told me I'd wind up in hell."

He felt a bony hand on his arm but couldn't move. The sound of a top popping on a beer can startled him as someone lifted his head.

"You drink this, boy," said Minnie Wissler. "You need fluids. It'll hep y'all build your blood back up. You done spilled most of it out that hole in your leg."

She put the can to his lips and poured some warm beer over them. Zip put his arm down and tried to raise himself up but every motion seemed to send daggers of pain shooting up from his wounded limb. Minnie poured in the beer and he gulped it down.

"That's it, Zipper Man," said Jamal from somewhere behind him. "Y'all gonna be drivin' trucks and makin' bucks before you know it."

Minnie pulled the can away when it emptied and Zip called for more. Then he asked, "Is my leg okay?"

"You ain't gonna be no mountain climber," the old woman muttered. "But you ain't dead."

"You was sho nuff tore up, Zip," said Jamal. "You real lucky you not dead."

"Guarantee you one thing," Zip grunted through clenched teeth. "The guys that did this are soon to be dead. Dead as their dead dog."

"Jamal, you drag his ass outta here. Make sure he takes all them pills. Give him Uncle Otis' hickory walking stick. It'll hep him get around."

Later at Jamal's apartment with the TV on Jamal said, "Hey, Zip, check it out, man," he pointed at the sketch of the Interstate Rapist suspect that filled the screen on his new fifty-inch color television. "Dude looks just like you. Get down. Too bad it's not you. You be famous."

Zip looked on, his jaw gaping. That was the afternoon he learned to walk again. He picked up that hickory stick, leaned on it and said, "Let's go. It's time I was home."

"So, go. Your van right outside."

"I can't drive."

"You don't expect me to carry your fat ass back to Dothan in your van and drive it back here, do ya?"

"Right. I can drive. Ouch. Help me down the fuckin' stairs." By the time he made it to the bottom step Zip had to catch his breath. The pain ripped through him causing sweat to bead up and trickle from his forehead. Slowly he worked his way to the van. Jamal half-lifted, half-pushed him into the driver's seat, slamming the door after him. Zip opened the window, slapped Jamal's hand. He wheeled the van slowly out into the street. The stiffness in his right leg kept him from using it for driving so he swung sideways again with it propped on the passenger seat. It made for awkward, jerky motions in the city driving with his left leg using the brake and the gas pedal. For days the van had sat locked up under the Alabama sun. Now Zip found the odor of rotting, blood-soaked carpet to be overwhelming, if not choking. Twice he stopped by the side of the road, leaned his head out the window and threw up.

Before leaving Montgomery, he pulled into a drive through liquor store and purchased two six packs of Pabst Blue Ribbon beer, two bottles of aspirin and a bag of ice before carrying on southbound. He pulled over and placed the bag of ice on the passenger seat, then lifted his bad leg onto the ice. Opening a Pabst, he washed down more aspirin tablets and screamed long and loud but it gave him no relief. The leg was on fire and he cursed that woman and her dog.

It was dark by the time he reached Dothan. Using the hickory stick he hobbled into the little house. In the darkness his bad leg seemed to bump every object in his way as he stumbled around. Still, he refused to burn a light until he closed himself in the bathroom. Leaning against the sink to take pressure off his leg he worked feverishly with scissors to remove as much of his hair as possible. Next, he lathered up his skull, working a razor from front to back to expose the pinkish skin. He struggled out of his clothes and stepped into a tepid shower. As the water reached his wounded leg he screamed in pain, vowing to kill the bitch that did this to him if he did nothing else.

After the shower he threw some fresh clothes and a bottle of Wild Turkey into a duffle bag, dragging it out to the van. One more trip inside to retrieve what cash he had stashed under the loose board in the front room floor. In minutes he was underway sporting a new look that made him all but invisible.

CHAPTER TWENTY-SEVEN

Carla took a swig of beer and studied the menu. "What's good here, Jack?" she asked.

"Most everything, save what they call Tex-Mex. So hot you won't sit on a truck seat next day. But if you ain't been home in a spell, try the barbecue pork sandwich."

"Is it good as Porky's?"

"Nothing's good as Porky's. But it's as close as you'll find anywhere north of the Mason-Dixon." He gazed into her eyes. "Damn, you look sweet."

"Shit. Next words out of that sorry mouth will be how much you miss me, followed closely by how tore up you are over dumping me."

He grinned and shrugged.

"Relax," she said. "You're here, you've got a pulse. Tonight, that'll do."

"I'd like to think I'm a little better qualified than that."

Now Carla shrugged and they both smiled.

After supper they strolled through the dark, potholed parking lot toward the far reaches where the yellow Kenworth sat next to Jack's black Mack. Carla slipped an arm through Jack's, steering him toward her truck. She stopped next to the driver's door, turned to face him and kissed his lips. Her arms snaked around his neck and tugged him close. "I'll open the other door for you," she whispered and kissed him again before releasing her grip.

97

Jack climbed in, sat in the passenger seat and whistled. "Mighty fine office you have here, Widow." He gazed around the cab, admiring its abundance of leather, wood-grain trim, and chrome. "Bet you have to work your sweet little tail off to make the payments."

"Don't you worry, Hon'. I saved you a piece."

"Uh-oh," Jack said, reaching for the stainless-steel cup in the second holder. "You have a co-driver. Let me guess. He's not with you this trip."

"Don't touch that."

He pulled back.

"That's my brother."

"Huh?"

"I mean, that was my brother's."

"Oh. Well. I'm sorry about your brother." He glanced out the windshield over the long, yellow hood. "No offense, Carla, but he sure made for some nasty news reports when he made his last run."

"When did you start believing everything you hear, Jack?"

"Are you saying he didn't do the things they said about him?"

"Yeah. That's what I'm saying." She looked down at her brother's cup. "That was a pack of lies the cops made up because they couldn't find the real killer. They knew Fish couldn't defend himself. He was dead. So, they just called him a killer and wrapped up this neat little package and sent it off to the TV and newspaper folks to cover their asses for killing the wrong man."

Jack nodded.

"You believe me, don't you?"

He looked out the window again and said, "Yeah. I reckon I do."

Carla smiled and stepped into the sleeper. Jack followed.

CHAPTER TWENTY-EIGHT

Rocky put in a full day of driving from Montgomery, stretching her allotted eleven hours rolling time just a smidgen to make it to Stony Ridge, south of Toledo. In the morning she would offload the clay early, reload and be on her way to Murfreesboro, Tennessee. Then she would run over to Knoxville to pick up Beau and off to the house for a much-needed vacation.

She wheeled into the truck stop and found a parking spot in the second row, relieved that she didn't have to sleep in the far reaches. Before she shut the diesel down an Ohio State Highway Patrol car pulled up in front of her truck, red and blue lights flashing. A trooper got out and walked to her door. She ran the window open.

"Shut it down, Miss," said the officer. "License and registration."

She handed them down. The trooper studied them with his flashlight, then handed them back.

"Ms. Steel, I need you to come with me. Lock your truck, step outside and keep your hands where I can see them."

"What's this all about?"

"Step outside now."

Rocky complied.

"Put your arms out to the sides." He patted her down.

"What do you want with me?"

He took her by the arm and led her to the patrol car.

"Where are you taking me?" She slid onto the back seat. The door closed behind her. The trooper got in and drove out of the parking lot and onto I-280 north. He made a radio call to report that he had suspect Roxanne Steel in custody.

"Suspect?" she said. "Suspected of what?"

"Ma'am, you are a suspect in the shooting of a police officer. I'm taking you to see the victim who is also witness to the shooting. If you're innocent he will clear you of the crime."

"Only if my luck changes. And thanks."

"For what?"

"For not cuffing me."

He nodded. In minutes they pulled into the emergency entrance of College Hospital in Toledo. The trooper escorted her into the building and walked her to L.T.'s room. L.T. was sitting up reading when they entered. He put his book down and greeted the trooper. Then he said, "You must be Rocky."

"And you must be L.T. Stafford," she said. "Will you please tell this officer that I didn't shoot you so that I can be on my way?"

"It's true," said L.T. "She's not the one."

"Great," she said, "I'm out of here."

The trooper raised an arm to stop her.

"Not exactly," said L.T.

"Why not?" said Rocky.

"Because of your encounters with the Interstate Rapist. He knows where you live."

"So?"

"So, you're being placed in protective custody by order of the FBI."

Rocky sighed. "What exactly is protective custody?"

"Well, ordinarily it means you would occupy a private cell in lockup until you're no longer at risk. In other words, for a time indeterminate."

"Aw, Christ," said Rocky. "Ordinarily. Is there a *but* in there?"

L.T. nodded. "If you agree you'll be released into my custody."

"In the hospital?"

"No. I'm being discharged in the morning. I'll be riding shotgun with you tomorrow and until we get this psycho bastard."

"Oh, hell no. No. No way."

"Suit yourself." He looked at the trooper. "Gifford, cuff her and take her away."

"Wait," she said. "I don't want to be in jail."

"It's jail," said L.T. "Or it's me."

"Rocky hung her head. "I'm just not accustomed to having company." She looked up at him. "I don't suppose you can drive a truck."

L.T. smiled. "I have some experience with that."

"Okay," she said. "I guess it's you."

CHAPTER TWENTY-NINE

Carla lay on her stomach, her head next to Jack's feet, peering at the television on the bureau as she surfed with the remote. Jack ran his fingers lazily over her naked buttocks causing goose bumps to add texture to their smooth contours.

"You were right," she said, without looking back at him. "That was damn fine barbecue. Now I'm thirsty."

"Me too. You want to go back inside and find the dance floor? Have a few cold ones?"

"Naw. I've got a case already chilled in the reefer. Let's go back and cool off. I worked up a sweat."

"I hear you." He popped up out of the berth, reached for his clothes on the floor and planted a kiss on her left buttock as he rose up again.

"You better kiss it, Jack."

"I'd like to be kissing it regular. What do you say? I'm a free man, now."

"Huh. Give you another chance to dump me? Think again."

"Okay, I was wrong. You gonna hold that against me forever?"

"No. Just until the day you die." She switched off the TV, got up and started dressing. When they were ready, she said, "Meet you around back." She climbed down and flipped open the outside door on the storage compartment beneath the sleeper, fished through her tool kit for the Crafters number 7 screwdriver just like the one she used to kill Arnold Perkins. Jack was swinging a barn door at the rear of the trailer when she got there.

"Where's the beer?" he asked, peering into the darkness of the enclosed van.

"To the right on the floor. You'll have to feel for it. You're good at that."

He chuckled and leaned in to reach for the beer. Carla stood close behind and with two hands raised the tool high above her head, ready to thrust.

"How can the cops get away with that?" asked Jack.

"With what?" She struggled to catch a breath, her heart pounding, hands shaking under the effects of adrenalin surging through her, setting nerves on fire.

"Blaming Marlin for those killings. Can't we do something about that? Get a lawyer maybe, or a private eye?" He dragged the beer box over to the door and plucked two cans from it. The screwdriver fell from Carla's hands and hit the ground with a clatter.

"What was that?" asked Jack.

"Huh?" she said, and brought her arms down as he turned around.

"That noise. Did you drop something?"

She bent down and picked up the tool and held it out for him to see under the pale glow from a parking lot light. "Can opener."

"Who needs a can opener?" he said, popping the top on a can.

"I do," she said, taking the unopened can from him. She held it on the trailer floor with one hand and slid the blade of the screwdriver under the ring on top of the can and pried it gently until it popped. "You see, I pay to have nails this nice," she said, raking them roughly across his cheek. "If I'm going to break them it'll be from doing something more fun than popping a top."

He grinned at her and sipped his beer. "Where you livin' now? Jack asked.

"Vero Beach."

103

"Vero. No shit? We're practically neighbors. I'm in Fort Pierce. I looked for y'all at the ranch. Found some new folks there. Been watchin' out for you. Hoped I'd run across you one day."

"You looked for me? Hah. Stopped getting it from your wife, I reckon. I must be next on the list. Look here, Jack. Don't think you can just come trucking back into my life for more than a night. I don't need the grief."

"What grief?"

"The grief I get when you go crawling on back to your wife, you snake."

"Carla, I swear, that was a big mistake. I swear, I know that now. She's out of my life for good."

"Well, I'm just not ready to buy that, Jack. If you want me, you're going to have to win me back."

"Sugar, I'd walk through fire for you."

"You may get your chance."

"What do you mean?"

"I mean, I've tracked down the no-good son of a bitch that killed my brother and I'm going after him."

"I thought the cops killed Fish."

"They did. But he didn't do the things they said. He was a good man. An honest driver."

"They said he was a killer. Cops don't just say that without evidence."

"Evidence. Jack, you are so naive. Dirty cops, Jack. Dirty cops create evidence. That cop from Ohio made up the evidence to get his ass out of a sling. He lied and the FHP just took his word for it and they killed Marlin."

Jack stared at her without speaking.

"I've got to get that bastard for what he did to us. He's a dirty cop and he'll pay." Tears began to flow from her eyes. "If you're smart, Jack, you'll just stay away from me and my trouble."

He clutched both her hands and gazed into her eyes. "I'll help you get him, Angel. I promise."

CHAPTER THIRTY

The next morning Ruby drove L.T. to the truck stop at Stony Ridge. They circled the parking lot until they spotted a yellow longnose with a stainless-steel reefer trailer.

"That's it," said L.T.

Rocky stood on the left step with window cleaner polishing the mirror glass.

"That's her?" said Ruby. "That's the woman you'll be with?"

"She's the only living witness of the Interstate Rapist. Relax Rube, I've got a job to do."

"Well Jesus, does she have to be so gorgeous?"

L.T. leaned over and kissed Ruby. "I'm old enough to be her father."

"Then she damn well better respect her elder or she'll be needing more protection."

L.T. got out and retrieved his travel bag from the back seat. Then he walked around to Ruby's door, leaned in the window and kissed her again.

"You better call me," she said. "And you better not be happy when you do."

L.T. walked over to where Rocky stood polishing the mirror. She looked down at him.

"You can stow your gear under the bunk," she said.

"Good morning to you too," said L.T.

105

"Hey, let's get one thing straight. We're not friends. I don't like this arrangement one bit. I'm only doing it to stay out of jail."

Ruby smiled and drove off.

L.T. settled into the co-driver seat and waited for Rocky. She finished up, climbed in and sat in the driver seat. Looking out through the windshield she said, "Just how much experience driving eighteen-wheelers have you had?"

"Not that much. I drove a Freightliner to Florida a few months ago. Since then, I acquired a student driver license so I'm legal to drive with you in the cab."

"Okay, I think I should start the driving. Have you got a log book?"

"In my bag."

"Get it and show the last seven days off duty. Then show three hours this morning unloading and reloading, then in the sleeper and we'll hit the road."

"But I didn't unload and reload and I'm not tired."

She looked at him and said, "You're in my world now and for much of my time, my life. Even though you're a cop I'm sure you've fractured a law or two. Just do it."

"Okay," he said and began writing in his log.

"We're hauling 28,000 pounds of auto parts," said Rocky. "That's a lighter load than usual so when it's your turn to drive you'll find she'll respond well. We're not out to set any speed records; we'll just obey the limit. We're going to Murfreesboro, Tennessee and we've got all day to get there."

L.T. nodded. In minutes they were out of the truck stop and rolling west on State Route 795. When they reached Perrysburg Rocky took I-75 south, worked her way up to speed and settled in the right lane, keeping her eye on the traffic ahead and behind.

Then L.T. said, "Rocky, why didn't you tell me about your husband?"

"Tell you what?"

"That your husband was murdered by the Iceman Killer."

She took her eyes from the road and said, "What? You believe the Iceman Killer murdered Nick?"

"I do."

"Well, no one else does." She looked at the traffic. "The FBI said it was a copycat and gave up investigating his death. Left it to the Indiana cops and they never ever found the killer."

"That's because the killer is not from or in Indiana. I believe the Iceman Killer is from Florida and I believe she is the woman who shot me."

"So that's why you thought it was me. I look like her and I'm from Florida."

"Not just that. I believe she drives a yellow longnose and goes by the handle 'Black Widow'."

Rocky stared at him a moment. "Oh my God," she said. "Black Widow. I met her. She drives a yellow Kenworth W900 with a stainless-steel Great Dane reefer just like mine. She killed Nick? She killed my husband? I had breakfast with her for Chrissakes."

"When and where?"

"A few days ago in Vero Beach, Florida."

"You didn't tell her who you are, did you?"

"No. Just Rocky."

"Good. We don't need two killers after you."

Rocky frowned and stared out the windshield. Then she said, "But you're after two killers."

He nodded.

"So am I," she said.

CHAPTER THIRTY-ONE

Zip slowed his van as he approached her house and cruised past looking for any sign she might be home. Neither the Peterbilt nor its trailer sat in the drive, just the Blazer. The place looked the same as it had the last time. Nobody home then. Nobody home now. He swung around, heading south, looking for a place to hole up while he kept an eye out for her. He thought about getting a room at the Pensacola Truck Stop, but truck stops had to be hot. They were on to him now – the sketch on the television proved that – making truck stops a likely place for them to look for him.

About fifty miles southeast he hit the Gulf Coast at Panama City Beach. The panhandle beaches couldn't boast the warm temperatures of South Florida, but tourists were beginning to roll into the area, with spring finally in the air. He found a mom-and-pop place called the Gulf Breezes Rest Inn that looked about half-full. He parked the van. Using the hickory stick he limped inside and tapped on the desk bell.

Laverne Moon waddled through an open door from her living quarters where she had been watching old reruns of Love Connection. Laverne and her husband Bill owned and ran the little motel. Bill happened to be out shopping for supplies according to Laverne. "What's wrong with your leg?" she asked. "How'd you get it messed up?"

"Gulf War," Zip lied. "I was a tank commander. Had Saddam himself pinned down until he got me with an anti-tank missile from out of nowhere. If I'd had air support that wacky Iraqi would've ate lead and I'd be rich and famous. But, no. No fly boys. Missile wiped out my whole crew. I only survived by my own will and determination."

"Shoot," said Laverne. "I reckon we better give you our special war hero rate of thirty-five dollars. Fill out the card." She pushed it toward him, along with a pencil.

"Appreciate it, ma'am. What's the regular rate?"

"Thirty-five dollars."

Zip signed the card as Leon Grouse of Hattiesburg, Mississippi. He counted out the cash, shaking his head. "Everybody's got a gimmick."

Laverne cocked her head to one side and studied his bare head. "You best have some sunscreen fer yer nut. Fry yer brain if you don't." She pulled a plastic bottle from a shelf behind her. Blowing the dust from it she placed it on the counter. "It's good stuff," said Laverne. "SPF fifty. Never burn with this concoction."

He took the bottle, stuffing it in his pocket.

"It's five dollars," said Laverne. She held out her hand.

Zip whipped out the bottle and dropped it in her hand. He took his key and limped out. The L-shaped motel sat opposite the beach, appropriately offering somewhat lower rates for not being on the water. Zip's room, about two-thirds down the far wing, faced the street, affording him a view of any approaching cops and the Gulf beyond. He kept the dark, paisley print curtains open about six inches to keep an eye out. Switching on the television, he tossed his duffle in a corner and popped the top on a can of beer.

CHAPTER THIRTY-TWO

L.T. and Rocky were north of Cincinnati when Rocky said it was time for a quick break. "There's a rest area at mile marker 27. I'll pull in there," said Rocky. "We'll stretch our legs."

"You're not going to try to escape custody, are you?"

Rocky smiled at him for the first time. "No. We both want these killers stopped. Besides, to be honest it's good to have company. I talk to Beau but he seldom answers back."

"Beau. That's your dog the hero."

She nodded. "We'll pick him up from the trauma center in Knoxville tomorrow after we unload."

"Hope he doesn't mind me being along."

"Me too."

It was a little after 8:00 pm when they pulled into the truck stop at Murfreesboro. Rocky found a spot in the second row and parked it for the night. "Let's grab a bite to eat," she said.

They went inside and found a booth. "Y'all want menus? Coffee?" a waitress asked, setting glasses of water before them.

Rocky nodded. Her smile faded. She looked at L.T. again and said, "So, you think this guy is after me, huh?"

"Can't say for certain. But if I was him, I would be."

"Somehow, I don't think that's meant as a compliment. But I have a surprise for him."

"This dirt bag is obviously very dangerous. From what I understand he's also provoked, given the size of the piece of leg he's missing. But his real problem is that someone can identify him. And that someone happens to be you."

She nodded.

"What did you mean when you said you had a surprise for him?"

"Nothing, really. I'd just love to get my hands on him."

"I hope you never have to. Maybe we'll get lucky. There's a good chance somebody will recognize him from the sketch that's going around. If that happens, he won't have time to worry about you. The FBI will make his full-time job avoiding capture." L.T. sipped his coffee.

"I know who he is," said Rocky.

L.T. almost choked. He put down his cup with a clatter. "You what?"

"I know where he lives, too. Lyle Crowder, Dothan, Alabama."

"You know him?"

"No. I know who he is."

"How could you know that?"

"He dropped his cell phone in my truck. I found it later and answered it when it rang. I found out his number and looked it up in a reverse directory on the Internet. I even went by his place in Dothan to see if he needed help dying from his leg wound."

L.T. stared at her, his jaw gaping.

Rocky shook her head. "I didn't go in. The place looked too creepy."

"We'd better be notifying the FBI."

"I really didn't want to do that."

L.T. couldn't believe it. "Why?"

"It's personal. Hey, you've never been attacked by a rapist so I don't expect you to understand. Sure, aside from a bump on the head I really wasn't hurt physically. But he got more personal than I ever want any creep to be with me. And he killed those other

111

women. He violated them and he killed them and he didn't even know them. You know, I've also got the knife he left in Beau's chest. And I wanted to return it. Personally."

"Revenge can get you killed, Rocky," he said.

"Revenge?" She sipped her coffee, put the cup down and shook her head. "Look who's talking about revenge. I call you in a hospital, worried because you're almost dead. You, you start attacking me, accusing me of shooting you and all out to get me. You wanted revenge."

"Guess it's a guy thing." He offered a weak smile.

"I don't care about revenge." She looked at the menu. "Okay, maybe a little bit. Maybe for what he did to Beau. But really, I guess I just want him stopped. And I'd love to be there when he's nailed."

"But that could take...who knows how long? Meanwhile, he's out on the street and takes a break from chasing you by taking down another innocent victim. Or worse, he gets to you when we least expect it and catches us with our guard down. It's just too dangerous. We can't leave this monster on the street. What if he kills someone else? You will always know you could have prevented it. How could you live with yourself?"

She sighed. "You're right. I don't know what I was thinking. This last couple of weeks has been...unusual. Should I call someone?"

L.T. fished his cell phone from the holster on his belt, flipped it open and called Chet's cell phone.

"Connor."

"Chet, it's L.T. I've got the name and address of the Interstate Rapist for you." He dictated the information.

"How did you get this?" he asked.

"I'm with Rocky. Roxanne Steel. You recall she had the great displeasure of meeting Crowder. Well, the guy lost his cell phone in her truck."

"We were sure due to get lucky on this one. I'll notify the FBI right away."

"Let me know when they get him."

"Thanks, L.T. Try not to piss her off again." He hung up.

"By the way," he said to Rocky. "How is Beau doing?"

"Much better. Looking just about as good as you."

L.T. smiled.

"One more thing. We haven't discussed sleeping arrangements."

"No discussion necessary. I'll sleep in the buddy seat. You have your normal sleeping quarters."

Rocky smiled.

CHAPTER THIRTY-THREE

Carla was offloaded and ready to leave Miami by noon the next morning. She talked to a broker and got a pickup order on a load of citrus for the next afternoon in Apopka, which meant she could spend the night at home in Vero Beach, head upstate in the morning. A night at home would be nice all right, but unfinished business awaited and this seemed a perfect time to see to it. Instead of cruising north on I-95 to Vero Beach she caught US27 for a quiet ride through the heart of the state.

Traffic on the latter proved to be sparse to nonexistent as she headed into sugar cane country, except for the odd cane hauler headed to or from one of several large refineries. She kept her speed below sixty, letting whatever happened to be heading in her direction to pass her easily. With the air conditioning off and the windows open wide she drew in the sights and smells of South Florida cane fields that stretched mile after mile. No houses marred the landscape, no towns, not even a gas station for the next fifty miles. Just pointed green leaves shooting skyward out of the rich, black muck.

Suddenly, the CB crackled and a raspy voice shook Carla from her reverie like an out of tune fiddle. "Grab hold of your doors, produce hauler. I'm fixin' to blow 'em off."

In the mirror she spied an old Autocar conventional of the seventies vintage with set-back front axle, the color of mushrooms before they're washed, blowing black smoke furiously as it struggled

OVERDRIVE

to overtake her truck. Gaining speed, the old tractor surged past her window then backed off to run alongside her, its longhaired driver wearing a grin as wide as the window.

"Flamin' cane fields, Batman," the driver called into the microphone. "It's Catwoman and she's smokin' her old man's Peter. Uh, that is, Peterbilt."

Carla waved a hand in front of her face, fanning the air and ran her window up. "It's not a Peterbilt it's a W9 and what the hell you burning in that thing, Batman? Your tights?"

"It's not Batman. It's Robin, the one with the big worm, darlin'. I'll tell you what's tight. My pants. You make my sticker peck out, Blondie. Whew. Is it hot in here, or is it just you?"

"Let me tell you something, Robin. This W9 ain't my old man's. It's all mine."

"Holy Batfuck, Batman. It's just as we suspected. She's a big city kitty. We better have a look at her bat cave."

Carla laughed. He was either a road comic – and she had run across a few – or pure psycho and it didn't particularly matter which. "You been on the farm too long, driver. You've got shit coming out every time your lips move."

"Go ahead, Catwoman. Insult me. I just can't get any respect. That fixes it. I'm going to the Chrome Shop and I'm gonna buy that shiny new chrome bumper then all the big city gals will respect me and throw their panties at me."

"No, they won't."

"Why not?"

"Because putting chrome on an old A-car is like putting perfume on a manure pile."

He laughed, a high-pitched, squealing laugh that made her reach for the volume button. "That's a good one."

"It's another insult, dummy."

"I knew that."

"Are you really called Robin?"

"Only by Batman."

115

"What's your handle, then?"

"Flat Out. They call me Flat Out."

"Is that because of the way you drive?"

"Nope. Because of the way I make love."

"Really?"

"Nope. My name's Melvin Flatt. Whenever you see me, I'm out. Flat Out. Get it?"

"I'm afraid to say no. You might try to explain it again."

The two trucks still ran side by side, each trucker shifting glances between the road and the other driver.

"What's your handle, Catwoman?"

"Catwoman will do for now. But don't think it makes me a pussy."

"Finally, we get to talk about pussy."

"Yeah. And you're flat out not getting any."

"Ooohh, me. That hurt. Guess we better change the subject, Batman. Catwoman, where you truckin' to?"

"Did you see that sign we just passed? It said north."

"I'm not scorin' a shitload of points here. Am I?"

"Depends. Since you're not really Robin, does that mean you lied about the big worm, too?"

"Hell, no. Wanna see?"

"Not if it's little."

"Hey, can I buy you a beer?"

"You see anything out here looks like a beer joint?"

"You got a point. Ain't even a gas station to pick up a six-pack."

"I got a case in the reefer. The unit's been off an hour or so but it should still be cool. And wet."

"Hell, let's get pulled over and get us a half-dozen."

"Unh-uh. I don't want to be seen on the side of the road by one of our other drivers. Know what I mean?"

"Yup. Y'all married."

Carla shrugged.

"There's a cutoff a few miles up on the right. It runs through the cane fields and dead ends at an old equipment shed. Nothin' but junk there now, nobody around. Lots of room to park and turn around, even dance naked. Follow me." He floored the Autocar and swung around in front of her, taking the lead in a cloud of black smoke.

"Hey, Flat Out. You ever been tied up?"

"Catwoman, I live to be tied up."

"Ever done it in a reefer?"

"Ask me tomorrow."

In minutes the old brown truck slowed to a crawl and turned onto a narrow, rutted road between two cane fields.

CHAPTER THIRTY-FOUR

Rocky and L.T. offloaded early, making it to the truck stop at Knoxville before noon Thursday. They took a taxi to the trauma center. L.T. waited in the cab. As Rocky entered the facility an attendant recognized her and brought Beau out of the care unit on a lead. He walked quietly at her side until he spotted Rocky, then picked up his head, prancing and tugging at the lead. The woman smiled and let go the tether. "That's the happiest we've seen him."

"Hello, Beau," said Rocky. "You old tough guy. My hero." She knelt down and hugged him.

"Dr. Churchill says no strenuous activity for two weeks, but definitely get him out exercising. Oh, and no jumping in and out of a truck for a couple weeks."

We'll behave, won't we, Beau?" He barked playfully, bobtail wagging. "Can he climb stairs?"

"I don't see why not."

Rocky led him out to the waiting taxi. She told the driver to take them to a hardware store and a fast-food drive-through. When they made it back to the truck stop, she opened the passenger door of the Peterbilt and set the bag of hot food on the seat. From the trunk the taxi driver removed a five-foot stepladder that Rocky purchased at the hardware store. Taking it from him she leaned it against the truck as a makeshift staircase up to the cab. She pulled a grilled chicken sandwich from the bag on the seat, took a bite and let Beau out of the taxi. Tearing off a small piece, she held

118

it out for him. It disappeared instantly. She placed another piece on the floor of the truck cab as Beau looked on. Rocky led him to the stair. Without hesitation he climbed the stairs retrieved the sandwich, stepped into the truck and sniffed at the bag. Rocky snatched up the sack. Walking away from the truck, she held the rest of the sandwich low at her side. Beau slipped down the steps, took the bait and sat down to eat it. L.T. looked on, amazed.

"You're just showing off, Beau Steel." She patted his neck. "Did I just teach you that? Something tells me you knew it already." She paid the taxi driver and put Beau back into the truck. "Let's see if we can get out of Tennessee before this storm hits." The breeze picked up, bringing with it a sudden chill.

A half-hour out of Knoxville Rocky switched on the lights and wipers. "Looks like the storm found us," she said to Beau, who lay stretched out on the floor in the sleeper. "Getting cooler, too." she said. By the time they neared Chattanooga Rocky let her speed drop as her knuckles whitened from gripping the wheel in heavy rain. At Forest Park just south of Atlanta she exited the Interstate and pulled into the State Farmers Market and parked.

"Time for supper," she said to L.T. "Grab the umbrella. We'll eat at the cafeteria. The fried chicken is the best I've had in America."

When their food arrived, they ate in silence. By the time they made their way across the parking lot the rain had stopped and the sun was slowly sinking. Beau was ready to stretch his legs. Rocky hauled out the ladder for him to make his way to the ground. She watched him with L.T. The reddish dog kept his distance, unsure what to make of the stranger.

"It's okay, Beau." She slipped an arm around L.T.'s waist and stood hip-to-hip with him. "He's a good guy. See?"

The dog went about his business. L.T. made no move. The arm and hip felt good.

Rocky said, "I don't want to go home tonight."

L.T. looked into her green eyes, held them for an awkward moment wanting suddenly to kiss her but unsure if it was the right thing to do. Then Beau sidled up to Rocky and she looked down and patted him.

"You're right. It'll be easier on us if we arrive in daylight."

Rocky pulled her arm away, walking toward the truck. Beau and L.T. followed. Rocky tossed the keys to L.T.

"Let's run down to Macon and find a place to sleep. You drive."

"You sure?"

"I trust you."

He climbed in behind the wheel as Rocky stowed the ladder. Beau headed for the sleeper.

L.T. whistled. "So, this is the legendary three-seventy-nine Peterbilt."

"This is it. The large car."

L.T. held the wheel a moment, gazing out over the long, flat hood. It had a squared-off appearance compared to Doobie's truck, which somehow gave it the impression of being muscular. "Don't mess with me" he mused, still peering straight ahead.

"Hmm?"

"It sort of says, 'Don't mess with me,' doesn't it?"

"I suppose it does," Rocky replied.

He looked around the cab, then leaned in the seat to view the sleeper compartment. The bedroom was by no means feminine. Still, Rocky had added a few items to give it a more lived-in look, including a couple of small wall hangings of landscapes. Beyond that, the abundance of leather, chrome and wood grain afforded a richness that wrapped around him, making him feel he could easily work or rest comfortably in these surroundings for long hours at a time.

Rocky briefed him quickly on the shift points for a Caterpillar engine, then slipped back into her quiet presence. She hadn't talked much since getting the news about Carla.

120

L.T. released the brakes, eased out of the parking area and made for the interstate. "The trailer's empty," he thought aloud.

"Vacation. Remember?"

He acknowledged with a nod, feeling he should be talking with her, drawing her into conversation and out of herself. But he struggled with what to say. She had been through so much in the past few months. The murder of her husband, being attacked by a vicious killer, then chatted up by the woman who killed her husband, even nearly losing her beloved dog, the one who saved her life.

CHAPTER THIRTY-FIVE

By the time darkness fell Zip had downed a couple more beers and a shot of Wild Turkey to ward off pain. He almost choked as his driver license picture appeared on the TV screen.

"Motherfucker," he said to the television. *That picture never did look a whole lot like me,* he thought. Still, he began to concentrate on what he might do to avoid capture. He slipped out quietly, rolled the van out onto the street and headed north again toward I-10, using SR81 to avoid traffic and cops. This time he forced himself to use the injured leg for driving. Needed to start loosening the muscles, for when he had to take on the woman. Bitch was going to pay.

Just over an hour later he turned onto I-10 east, drove to the Ponce de Leon rest area and parked in a dark corner among the pine trees. He watched as a minivan with a half-dozen students in it parked not far from him. The gang piled out and headed for the rest rooms. Zip took his screwdriver and hobbled as quickly as he could. He had the tag off in no time, making his way back to his van. In a minute the kids piled back in and took off, unaware they were driving without a tag.

Zip sat patiently waiting for his next victim. The idea was to steal another tag, leaving the first stolen in its place. That would slow down the cops. They would be looking for a minivan with the stolen tag, figuring the driver had just made an exchange. But then to his surprise a real opportunity afforded itself. A tow truck pulled in dragging an accident-damaged Chevy pickup. Before the driver made it to the john, Zip had the tag off the wreck and was installing the stolen one from the minivan onto the damaged vehicle. After the truck pulled out, he slapped the Florida tag on his van, ditching his Alabama tag in a garbage can and smiling from ear to ear.

The Peterbilt sounded and felt different than Doobie's truck. The twin chrome stacks gave a mellow rumble to the Caterpillar's drone that was not at all unpleasant or overpowering. It added to the truck's overall feel of strength. He could get to like this feeling. The rig was up to speed in no time and felt as easy to drive as any car. L.T. sensed that it was as nimble under heavy load as it was drawing an empty.

Rocky worked at her log in her seat on the passenger side. Finally, she spoke. "First impression?"

"Of you or the truck?"

"Interesting opportunity," she said. "But let's stick with the truck for now."

"It's easy to see why you do this. Your office is much more impressive than mine." Then he added, "And Doobie's."

Rocky smiled. "Glad you like it."

"Rocky, I hope I'm not intruding."

"Intruding?" She took a deep breath. "Under different circumstances that might well be the case. Right now, I'm happy to have the personal security service. It feels good. Feels like I might sleep tonight."

"You have trouble sleeping?"

"Lately, yeah. When Nick died it was a bit of an adjustment. I mean, true we were always on the road and going in different directions so we didn't see a whole lot of each other. But it was good to know he was never more than a phone call away. Since he's been gone, it's like it's me against the world. It helped a bit when Beau showed up a few weeks ago. But since we met this pervert, I've been afraid to shut my eyes. Seems like when I do all I see is that twisted bastard's face staring down from above me." She shivered.

"How long were you married?"

"Not long, really. Just short of six years. Nick came rolling up out of Texas in this big old fancy truck and blew past me on the interstate in Michigan and the rest is history."

"Were you originally from Michigan?"

"Yep. Born and raised in General Custer's hometown."

"Monroe? That's not far from where I grew up." He twisted his hands around the leather-covered steering wheel. "It's none of my business but did you love your husband?"

"You're right. It's none of your business. But yes, like a fool, I did."

"Why like a fool?"

"Well, it was great at first, we got along like the best of friends. And I suppose we were still pals when the end came but there was always this tension between us, like background noise kind of that's never really gone. The pressures of being on the road and apart so much. And the money. There just never seemed to be quite enough of it. I knew he was fooling around and I hated it. Still, I liked the guy and yes, probably loved him. I miss him."

"I'm sorry."

"Thanks. So, to make a long story short, no you're not intruding. Having you around is sure to help me sleep."

"I'm not sure I like hearing that from a beautiful woman."

She blushed. "That's not what I meant and you know it."

CHAPTER THIRTY-SIX

L.T. parked the tractor-trailer at a motel on the outskirts of Macon. He looked at Rocky. "I can sleep out here if you'd feel better," he said.

"No. I need to know you're right there to protect me. I told you before. I trust you."

He nodded. Rocky went inside to rent a room. L.T. got the ladder for Beau. The dog came down the ladder neatly and trotted toward the grassy edge of the parking lot. L.T. followed him. When Beau finished, he wandered up to L.T., bobtail wagging. L.T reached down to pat his neck but the dog pulled back and sat down as Rocky returned with a key.

"That's not very neighborly, Beau Steel. I told you he was a good guy."

The dog looked at her, cocking his head to one side.

"What?" she asked. "You're jealous?" She looked at L.T. "Guess he's not going to respect you until you save my life or something."

He grabbed their bags, locking the truck as they headed for the room. Setting a bag on each bed he sat down and slipped his shoes off. Beau lay on the carpet between the two beds.

Rocky said, "I'm going to get a shower."

L.T. nodded. Stretching out on the bed he found the television remote and started surfing channels. In a few minutes Rocky was back, clad in a pale blue cotton nightie, her short, wet blonde hair brushed straight back behind her ears. He thought she had the cutest little ears.

"Which bed would you like?" he asked.

"You're fine where you are," she said. "But I need to ask a favor."

"Name it."

"I'm scared," she said. "No, I'm really scared. This bastard has me totally spooked. He has me thinking my life is about to end."

"Don't worry. I'm not going to let anything happen to you."

"Shut up and listen," she said. She smiled weakly. "Sorry. I'm trying to ask something here and I don't quite know how to say it. I've been alone for a while now. And I'm shit-scared."

He was sitting up now, listening intently.

"Look, here it is. I need somebody to hold me, just hold me, tonight. And I need it to be you."

Without saying a word, he stood up, took her in his arms, feeling the warmth of her nearly naked body, her breasts pressed against his chest, face on his shoulder. Gently, he combed his fingers through her hair, feeling the cool dampness. His other hand reached behind him to douse the light. Then he held her for several minutes in the soft glow of the television. After a while they moved to the bed. She lay her head on his chest as he slipped an arm around her and they watched TV.

Rocky's eyes began to get heavy. She rose up and said, "Sorry. Why don't you grab a shower? I'm fine, now."

He pressed his lips gently to her cheek, then rose, took his bag and disappeared into the bathroom. A few minutes later he emerged wearing gym shorts and a t-shirt. Rocky, in bed now, reclined against two pillows, watching television through half-open eyes. She had turned down the other bed for him so he slipped into it quietly. In minutes he could hear her breathing become deeper. He glanced over to see that she was sleeping soundly. Switching off the TV he settled in for the night, but couldn't seem to sleep, a familiar situation to him the last few years.

His mind went to work at reviewing events of the last couple of weeks. He tried to keep it clinical, examining the facts, searching for clues. But so much had happened he found it difficult to concentrate at times. Ego kept jumping in with the gloves off, throwing punches. He thought for a time about the Interstate Rapist. What did he really know about him? Very little, aside from his name and address as provided by Rocky. Lucky thing she had not wanted to arrive home in the dark. He'd been so caught up in other things he was about to rush headlong into a confrontation with a killer without doing any homework at all. He concluded it was time for a chat with the Florida Highway Patrol. About Carla Sears and Lyle Crowder.

He was dozing, slipping in and out of light sleep sometime after three when he awoke to the tickle of fingers tracing lightly through the hairs on the left side of his chest, purposely avoiding the area of his surgery. The dim light filtering in around the curtains made her blonde hair glow. He slipped an arm around her to find that she was no longer wearing the nightgown. His fingers traced soft circles in the small of her back. She slid her hand from his chest across his flat stomach and beyond until she held him in her hand and slowly stroked. He tugged her closer until he felt the silky curls of her pubic hair against his thigh. His breath quickened.

"Rocky," he whispered. "I'm old enough to be-."

She brought her fingers to his lips. "My lover," she said. No more words were spoken. He kissed her softly at first, heating quickly and growing passionate. They made love slowly and with tenderness, gradually building toward mutual satisfaction.

In the morning L.T. awakened to find Rocky still curled up under his arm, her head on his shoulder. It was the first time he remembered waking with a smile on his face.

In minutes Rocky began to stir. "Mmm," she said, without lifting her head from his chest. "Know something, L.T.?"

"Yep," he replied. "You are absolutely gorgeous."

"True. But that's not it."

"What?"

"When you're not pissed off at me, you're really a sweet man to be with."

He kissed the top of her head.

"It is so nice to wake up without an alarm going off," said Rocky.

"Having a naked blonde in bed with you isn't bad either."

She popped up and kissed him quickly on the lips, then headed for the bathroom. L.T.'s eyes locked on to her naked buttocks, watching them wiggle as her hips swayed. In minutes she emerged fully dressed, to his disappointment. Rocky took Beau out for a walk while L.T. dressed. She returned with coffee for two.

"You are an angel," said L.T. "But that dog of yours still won't have anything to do with me."

"Hmm," she said. "I wonder if he knows something I don't."

"After last night you know pretty much everything about me."

"Likewise. Say, you want to get out of here?"

He sipped the coffee and nodded. "You driving?"

"What's wrong with you?"

"I need to make a couple of phone calls."

"In that case, allow me."

CHAPTER THIRTY-SEVEN

Zip rolled out of bed still in his clothes, grabbed the hickory walking stick and went shopping. At the Walgreen's he picked up a fresh supply of surgical gloves, having forgotten to bring the box from the house. In a military surplus store, he found a combat vest in which he could conceal a couple of small but very sharp knives. The storekeeper wanted to sell him a gun but Zip told him he was just going on one of those paint ball weekends and wouldn't know how to use a real gun. The guy seemed to buy it. Zip's longtime weapon of choice was a large hunting knife that he liked to carry in a sheath on the side of his right boot but his leg was still so swollen he couldn't wear the high-top engineer boots. And he didn't want to buy another weapon in the surplus store in case it might make this dude feel the need to tip off the cops. Instead, he headed for a pawnshop where he located a suitable blade, a nice eight-incher from L.L. Bean with wooden handle that fit his grip like it was made for it. Next stop was a liquor store to pick up more pain medicine. Finally, in a hardware store he found a honing stone for sharpening the blades to razor quality. Soon he would be ready.

When his arsenal was finally organized, he loaded everything into the van and headed for DeFuniak Springs. Slowly he cruised along SR83. From about a quarter-mile away he caught sight of a car in the driveway but couldn't make it out through the trees. As he drew to within a couple hundred yards, he spied a blue light on the car's roof. Immediately he wheeled the van around and headed back toward Panama City Beach. Instead of going to the motel he stopped off at a sporting goods store, wandering around inside until he found a display of crossbows.

"Goin' huntin'?" asked a red-haired, red-faced young man named Jeffery.

"Naw," said Zip. "Got a 'possum problem at the trailer."

"Y'all don't need that for 'possums. We got poison. Whole lot easier."

"Give yer head a shake, boy. No don't, it'll probably rattle." He chuckled. "Poison 'em, they crawls in a hole in the wall and dies. Stinks to high heaven. Spoils the smell of a good beer fart."

The clerk laughed too. Zip bought a crossbow and supply of carbon steel-tipped arrows and headed back to the motel. Jeffery said those arrows would go right through body armor without slowing down. With the cops hanging around he would have to change his strategy, make his move at night.

L.T.'s cell phone rang. He patted his pockets until he found it, leaning to one side to retrieve it from his trousers.

"L.T.," he said.

"L.T. Stafford?"

"Yeah, go ahead."

"Chief Stafford, this is Detective Tom Hardman of the Florida Highway Patrol."

"What can I do for you?"

"I understand you were involved in solving a homicide that occurred outside a truck stop in Wildwood, Florida last year."

"That's correct. What is it you need to know?"

"In light of recent events we are taking another look at the homicide of Arnold Perkins."

"What recent events?"

"Well sir, another body was discovered in the parking area of that same truck stop early this morning."

OVERDRIVE

"Another homicide?"

Rocky looked over at him.

"I'm afraid so. Correct me if I'm wrong. The Perkins killer was also responsible for a homicide in your jurisdiction. Isn't that right?"

"Yes. The Iceman Killing. A truck driver was found frozen stiff on a seventy-degree day. You think this latest homicide is in some way connected?"

"Definitely. We've got a frozen truck driver here on an eighty-degree day."

"Did you say frozen?"

"That's not all. It's a signature killing. And the signature is L.T. Stafford. What do you make of that?"

"What do you mean? How did you connect it to me?"

"Perkins was killed with a screwdriver as I recall."

"That's right. A Crafters number seven."

"Our victim was in possession of a Crafters number seven."

"Jesus. The same truck stop. The same screwdriver. And frozen."

"Yeah. And your name is carved in the handle of this screwdriver. What do you figure that means?"

"I know exactly what that means. It means the real Iceman Killer is still out there and she wants me to know it."

"Did you say she?"

"Unh-huh."

"I'd really like to interview you further, Chief Stafford. I don't suppose there's a chance you'll be in Florida soon."

"In fact, I'm on my way to Florida this minute. Though, I don't think I'll be in your area."

"Where are you heading?"

"Ever heard of DeFuniak Springs?"

"Oh, yeah. It's over yonder on the panhandle. What's over there?"

131

"I have reason to believe the Interstate Rapist will be there to try to finish off his last victim, the one that got away."

"Do what?"

"I'm traveling with Roxanne Steel, the woman who identified the rapist. She's the only eyewitness and he knows where she lives."

"You're on your way there now?"

"Yes. We'll arrive late this afternoon. Do you think you could have some people there? We could use the help."

"I'm sure we can spare some officers for that worthy cause. In fact, I may try to get up there myself to have that chat. Have you notified the FBI?"

"No. Could you take care of that? I think they're more likely to take you seriously."

"Done. Let me ask you something pertaining to our latest Wildwood case. You said you thought the Iceman Killer is a woman. What can you tell me about her?"

"Her name is Carla Sears, sister of Marlin, the dude we nailed for the Iceman and Perkins killings, among others."

"What makes you suspect her?"

"She's a truck driver. She loved her brother. And she shot me last week not far from my townhouse. She went there to kill me."

"Determined, isn't she?" he said. "So, she wants revenge for the killing of her brother."

"Looks that way, yes."

"Your townhouse is in Ohio, right?"

"Yes."

"She traveled a long way to bag your ass. Did you notify State or local police last night?"

"Yes, the Ohio State Highway Patrol is watching out for her."

"I see. And this woman is the one who shot you?"

"I believe so."

"Sounds to me like you're on the shit lists of a couple of dangerous individuals."

OVERDRIVE

"I suppose I am. But that doesn't make me a bad person. Just popular. I'll call you when we're about to arrive at the witness' residence." He hung up.

"We're in a lot of trouble, aren't we?" said Rocky.

"I suppose we are. But at least we know where it's coming from. We'll do our best to make ready for it."

CHAPTER THIRTY-EIGHT

Just south of Cordele, Georgia, Rocky took the ramp for SR300 to Albany. L.T. busied himself with his notebook, reading, jotting, asking the odd question aloud to himself. He turned to Rocky and asked, "How bad was Crowder wounded? How bad was his leg?"

"Really bad. Beau took a nasty chunk right out of his calf muscle. I've never seen anything like it. Had to be the size of an orange."

"He would have needed medical attention. Maybe even surgery. I wonder if they checked hospitals and clinics in the area after your attack."

"The Tennessee State Trooper said they would do that. They were all over it right away, looking everywhere for him."

"How the hell does a guy like that get away?" He shook his head, gazing out the window. "You know, there's a good chance he didn't. For all we know he may have just crawled off somewhere and bled to death."

"Shit. That's right. I never thought of that. I cleaned a lot of blood out of here. Most of it was his. And his place in Dothan looked deserted. I'll bet that's why. I'll bet he just up and died."

"FBI is probably checking his house right now. It'll be a while before we can find out what they learn there."

"Unless we go to his house ourselves."

L.T. nodded. "We need to know what the FBI knows before we go rolling in to your place."

134

"We might be doing all this worrying for nothing." She chewed her lip, not really ready to believe they were home free. "We'll know soon enough. We're only three hours from Dothan and heading straight for it."

"Why are we going to Dothan, Alabama?" he asked.

"It's on the way to my place. You might as well see how he lives."

L.T. nodded.

Rocky took SR62 west out of Albany, winding their way through the gently rolling hills of South Georgia. L.T. watched her work, shifting gears, wheeling the massive rig around winding turns as the two-lane blacktop weaved its way through dense pine forests broken occasionally by the odd pecan grove.

It amazed him the way she seemed to handle the truck so effortlessly. When driving the Freightliner Doobie's entire body would shift as he jammed the stick into gear, relying more on muscle than technique. But with Rocky it was pure finesse, every move as gentle as if she were placing pearls on a pillow. Her torso rarely moved, arms and legs did everything. And the truck responded fluidly, never jerking, never lugging, never laboring. It was as if that Peterbilt was another part of Rocky herself. He liked the gentle nature of this woman.

When they reached Dothan, they parked at the truck stop. Beau needed a walk so they all stretched their legs a bit. After a quick lunch Rocky called a taxi. She and L.T. rode over to Crowder's house next to the railroad yard.

When the cab pulled up, police and FBI vehicles parked around the house, lights flashing. A small crowd of onlookers hung outside the tape that surrounded the yard of the small frame house. Rocky and L.T. stepped out, telling the driver to wait. L.T. pushed his way through the crowd with Rocky in tow. He approached a uniformed officer standing just inside the tape, showed his badge and asked to speak with an FBI agent. The young man disappeared into the house, returning momentarily with a man in a gray business suit.

"I'm Agent Jeb Hickman of the Montgomery Field Office," he said

"L.T. Stafford." He extended a hand and they shook.

"Stafford. Stafford. L.T. Stafford." He nodded. "Yeah. You the one that closed that Iceman thing last year?"

"That would be me."

"Pleased to meet you. You aware it's reopened?"

He nodded. "I heard they found another victim in Wildwood."

"Sure enough. Is that why y'all are here?"

"No." He pointed to Rocky. "This is Roxanne Steel, the only living eyewitness of the Interstate Rapist and the one who identified him as Lyle Crowder of this address."

"Ma'am," said Agent Hickman. "You're one lucky woman. So, what can I do for y'all?"

"We're on our way to Ms. Steel's residence," said L.T. "Crowder knows where she lives. We were hoping you could tell us he hasn't been here recently, that maybe he crawled off and died after Ms. Steel's dog took a piece of him."

"I see. You know, of course, that I'm not at liberty to disclose any information about evidence found here or elsewhere."

"I was hoping you could just let us know one way or the other without compromising your investigation."

The agent nodded. "Between you and me, we found bloodstained gauze in the bathroom, which indicates two important facts. One, he was able to get medical help without us knowing it; and two, he's mobile. Looks like he cleaned up here sometime in the last few days."

"And he hasn't been apprehended yet?"

"That's correct."

"I was afraid of that," said L.T. "Thank you Agent Hickman."

Back in the cab Rocky asked, "We don't know for certain he's after me, right?"

"No. It just seems the logical thing for him to do. Assuming a serial killer has a logical side to his diseased mind. If you'd rather not go to your place we could avoid it, hope he makes a move and the cops catch him."

"I've been thinking about that. But if they don't catch him," she took a breath, looking out the window. "Then it never ends. I can't imagine going through life wondering what rock this son of a bitch is going to crawl out from under, what door he'll be waiting behind just to torture me to death. If we don't end this now, I have no life."

L.T. slipped an arm around her and she slid close, her head on his shoulder. At the truck stop L.T. phoned Detective Hardman and let him know they would arrive at Rocky's in a couple hours. He indicated there were already officers watching the house.

"You drive," said Rocky. "My mind is elsewhere."

"Aren't you concerned mine will be too?"

"Unh-uh. You're a veteran cop. You've seen stuff like this before."

"That I have," he said, climbing into the driver's seat.

In minutes the rolling swells of the southern Alabama countryside began to rise and fall beneath him as the Peterbilt chewed them up and asked for more. Even without a load the yellow truck hugged the road in the turns and made him want to accelerate each time it emerged from a bend. The ride was smooth and crisp, the steering precise, making him smile uncontrollably as though wheeling a Lamborghini through a challenging road course. Rocky had grown quiet. Still, she couldn't take her eyes off him as he played at working. For a few minutes, at least, it offered a little respite stolen from their troubled lives.

Too soon they reached DeFuniak Springs and rolled on to Rocky's house. She pointed out her place as they approached, telling him to pull off on the grassy shoulder. A Florida Highway Patrol car sat in the drive with two officers standing in the yard chatting. They watched the big rig park, the hissing of its air brakes cutting the stillness of the north Florida afternoon.

L.T. and Rocky climbed down. Rocky got the ladder and let Beau out while L.T. greeted the officers.

"How do, Mr. Stafford," said one. "We hear you're the man bagged Marlin Sears over to Gainesville last year."

L.T. nodded. Changing the subject he said, "Seen anything of Crowder?"

"No sir. That ole boy have to be a fool to show his sorry self here. We'll nail his ass to a pine tree."

"The way I see it," L.T. said, looking around. "He's not known for being overly intelligent. I believe he's got reason to be in the area. And to come here."

"There will be folks here waiting on him if he does. Round the clock."

Rocky walked over with Beau. "You gentlemen hungry? I could fix something."

"Coffee would be appreciated, ma'am."

"Coffee it is," said Rocky. "L.T., walk me inside."

L.T. nodded and led the way. They entered through the front door into the living room. The two-by-four still jammed the damaged rear door shut rendering it inaccessible from outside. They gave Beau the run of the house. The dog wandered throughout but remained calm, sniffing here and there without finding anything to excite him. Satisfied there was no immediate threat of danger Rocky headed for the kitchen to start a pot of coffee brewing. L.T. dropped the bags in the master bedroom.

"L.T.," called Rocky. "Were you ever fired from a job as a carpenter?"

He joined her in the kitchen. "What is that devious mind of yours getting at?" he asked.

"I have a door that needs fixing." She pointed to the board holding the door closed.

138

L.T. glanced at it then gazed out the kitchen window at the stand of pines beyond the yard. "Pretty place you have here, Rocky."

"I'll take that as a no. Guess I'll have to call somebody."

He shrugged. "I've just never been good with my hands."

"All evidence to the contrary," she said, walking over and slipping her arms around him. "I'm so glad you're here."

He kissed her lips softly. "So am I," he said. They held each other as the coffee brewed.

CHAPTER THIRTY-NINE

Later that evening L.T. became restless as a sudden stillness settled over the place. He walked to the front door, saw the officer standing sentry in the yard and went out to chat with him.

"Evening, sir," said the trooper. "Everything all right?"

L.T. nodded. "I was about to ask you the same thing."

"Right quiet night."

"Where's your partner?"

"Out back. Only two ways to approach the property. From the road in front or through the pines out back. We've got it covered."

He went back inside. Rocky had something on television but wasn't really watching it. "I feel like a prisoner," she said. "I feel like I can't go anywhere or do anything for fear that maniac will get me. I've never felt this way before. Now I'm a prisoner in my own home. I can't stand it. It's not fair."

"Try to relax," said L.T., taking a seat beside her on the sofa.

"How can I relax? How can you?" She stood up and wandered about the room trying to overcome the feeling of helplessness.

"It's getting late," said L.T. "Why don't we try to get some sleep?"

Rocky nodded. They headed for the bedroom. Beau curled up on the floor beside the bed, watched them as they undressed in silence. Rocky donned flannel pajamas and slipped beneath the covers. L.T. switched out the light and peered out the window. He spotted the second trooper standing in the yard facing the trees.

140

Beyond him the truck and trailer sat next to the shed, illuminated by a single light over the door to the building. He pulled back the covers and got into bed next to Rocky. Without hesitation she slid over and lay her head on his shoulder. Despite the tension and the pain in his chest he felt better than he had in a long time.

Sometime later he awakened with a start. Beau was prancing back and forth in the bedroom without making a sound. L.T. peered out the window.

"What is it?" asked Rocky, sitting up.

"Can't see the cop," he said. "Now that's weird. The light is out on the barn, but there's a light on in your truck."

"Jesus," said Rocky. "He's here." She picked up the phone but it was dead.

"I'm going outside." He flipped the light switch but nothing happened. "I don't suppose you have a gun."

"Unh-uh," she replied. "Take Beau with you. He won't take any shit off that creep. I know he's ready to get back at that killer."

"I won't take any shit off Crowder either." He tugged on his jeans and fished the cell phone from his shirt. "Come on, Beau," he said. The dog followed. L.T. felt his way to the front door and stopped to look out. The other trooper was nowhere to be seen. Rocky worked her way to the kitchen, rummaged through a drawer until she found a cigarette lighter, then used it to light a candle.

"Hold on," she said. She retrieved her travel bag from the bedroom. In a moment she produced a flashlight from it and handed it to L.T.

"That's obviously not just for carrying your work clothes."

"You'd be surprised what a girl can pack in a bag like this."

L.T. and Beau went out the door, following the beam of the flashlight. Rocky returned to the bedroom. She placed the candle on her nightstand, stuffed clothing under the bed covers and retreated into the open closet with her travel bag. Crouching in a darkened corner, she removed a can of starting fluid from the bag. She tugged the top from it with a popping sound. Reaching in again she came out with Crowder's hunting knife which still bore the bloody stains from Beau's wound. Her hands shook; her breath came in short, quick gasps as she tried to settle in and wait for the hunter.

Outside, Beau led L.T. to the trooper who lay face down in the front yard, an arrow from a crossbow protruding from his back. He checked for a pulse but found nothing. Reaching under him he felt for the microphone of his portable radio but it had been cut clean off. L.T. flipped open his cell phone, punched 911 and waited. No service. He took the sidearm from the dead man's holster and moved toward the rear of the house. Beau found the second officer sitting against the back wall of the house. L.T shone the flashlight on him. His eyes stared blindly into the night, an arrow buried in his chest. L.T. turned and crept toward the Peterbilt with Beau at his side.

From the closet Rocky heard the floor creak in the hall outside her bedroom. Her breathing stopped as she tried to listen but her heart pounded like a Cummins piston on a winter morning. She tried to crouch lower in the corner. It creaked again and she wanted to scream but no sound came out. In the soft glow of the candle, she caught sight of his dark form inching into the room. His face remained in the shadows. She wanted to lunge with the knife, bury it in his chest or back, but couldn't be sure it was him. And then she saw him limp toward the bed, his right leg dragging somewhat behind the other. It could only be Lyle Crowder, the Interstate Rapist. She clutched the knife in one hand, twisting the bone handle in her slender fingers. Her other hand wrapped tightly about the spray can, a finger on the button ready to dispense the paralyzing mist. She ached to spring out at him. Everything was right. But she couldn't seem to move a muscle. His arm rose slowly as he inched toward the bed. She caught the glint of steel from his weapon rising above his head. Suddenly he grunted a low, gravelly sound and plunged the knife through the lumpy clothing into the mattress.

Rocky screamed and leaped up from the floor of the closet. Zip wheeled to face her. She pointed the ether can at the candle and let loose its spray. The blinding light from the flame caught him off guard and he froze momentarily. She swung the fiery spray in his face, singing his eyebrows and knocking him backward. Rocky lunged, plunging the hunting knife into his belly to the hilt. He swung a meaty backhand and sent the makeshift flamethrower clattering to the floor. Its fire died instantly. He looked down at the knife protruding from his gut and said, "I been looking for that."

Rocky pulled the knife out. Ready to stab again but Zip's right hand caught her by the throat, almost lifting her from her feet. His other hand went up over his head, ready to bury his new L.L. Bean knife. She struggled to breathe but could draw no air, his giant hand clamping off her windpipe. Her eyes began to roll backward, her body burning its last few molecules of oxygen. She was slipping into cold, wet darkness, a hollow tomb between two worlds.

Somewhere far away the sound of breaking glass barely reached her. Beau flew through the window with a crash, leaped into the air and attached himself to the meaty arm holding Rocky's throat. Zip screamed a piercing wail. Blood ran from Beau's mouth as his jaws clamped the muscles of Zip's forearm, penetrating flesh. Zip stared at the blood running from his arm. In the dim light it looked blackish and hideous. He began to tremble and lost his grip on Rocky.

She fell into a crumpled heap in the closet. Zip swung his knife in the direction of Beau's head. The razor-sharp blade struck a glancing blow to the dog's solid skull, slicing the skin but rendering little real damage. Beau held fast. Zip raised the weapon again, took aim at the fleshy part of Beau's neck. A shot rang out. Zip stumbled, swung with the knife but before it landed, another shot sounded from outside the window. Then another. The big man shuddered, dropped the knife and spun around, the dog still dragging from his bloody right arm.

L.T. leaned in the window, leveled the gun and fired a final shot into Zip's forehead. Instantly he crashed to the floor like a felled pine tree. Beau released Zip's arm and stood guard over the lifeless body. L.T. climbed through the broken window and moved straight to Rocky. He lifted her limp body from the closet, lay her on the bed and immediately began CPR.

"Come on, Rocky," he grunted, but she did not respond. He kept working on her. "Come on, damn it."

Beau barked sharply. Suddenly Rocky coughed and began breathing on her own. In a moment she opened her eyes, rubbing her throat to ease the pain. She looked up at L.T., then over at Beau. "Thank God you guys are okay. You are, okay?"

"Yeah. Are you okay?"

"Yeah. What about Crowder?"

"Dead."

"Thanks, L.T."

"For what? You and Beau had him on the way down, I just helped him the rest of the way."

"Sure," she said. "Help me up."

"Stay where you are," he said, flipping open his cell phone again. He punched 911. This time it worked. "I'm getting an ambulance for you."

"I'm fine."

"I want a second opinion on that. You were on death's door a minute ago. I had to give you mouth-to-mouth."

"Did you do anything else? I feel like I want a cigarette."

"You don't smoke. Hello," he said into the phone. "This is L.T. Stafford. I'm at the residence of Roxanne Steel. You've got two FHP officers down, here. They're both dead. We need an ambulance and a crime scene unit. The Interstate Rapist is also dead." He hung up. L.T. fetched a towel from the bathroom and dabbed at the wound on Beau's head.

144

"Oh no," said Rocky. "He's hurt."

"That's not hurt. He's tougher than me. Don't worry about him, he'll be fine. I'll get him stitched up in the morning."

Sirens sounded in the distance. In minutes the place was crawling with cops, FBI agents and paramedics. The ambulance carried Rocky to hospital in Pensacola, two hours away. L.T. wanted to go with her but he stayed behind to find help with Beau's injury. He managed to wake up a veterinarian at Fort Walton Beach and by six-thirty in the morning had Beau in Rocky's Blazer for the ride over.

CHAPTER FORTY

By eight-thirty L.T.'s cell phone was ringing nonstop. Whenever he would flip it closed it immediately rang again. The first call came from Chet Connor as police forces throughout the country received word that Lyle Crowder, suspect in the Interstate Rapist murders was shot dead by L.T. Stafford of White Falls Police Department in Ohio.

"Congratulations, hero," said Chet.

"Lucky's more like it," L.T. said.

"I didn't believe that when you got Sears and I don't believe it now. Some guys work all their lives dreaming of knocking a bad guy off the most wanted list. You've done it twice in less than a year. The odds against that happening are higher than Jupiter. Stop being modest and bask in the glory. You've earned it."

"Thanks, Chet."

"Is everybody okay?"

"Two FHP officers died. Rocky's in the hospital but she'll be fine. I've got her dog at a clinic right now getting him patched up. As for me, aside from being sore all over from this damn chest wound I'm fine."

"Sorry about the two troopers. Glad to hear the rest of you are all right. Now, get your ass back up here and get to work. Take care, my friend. Nice work." He hung up.

In the next few minutes L.T. fielded calls from Detective Hardman of the Florida Highway Patrol, the deputy director of

146

the FBI, two news reporters and a television producer. Doobie called to tell him not to get a big head over it. Then Carla Sears called again.

"I hear you're still killing people and getting away with it," said Carla.

"I hear you are, too. Another poor slob in Wildwood. You gave yourself away when you signed my name to it."

"I was sending you a greeting card. Sounds like you got it."

"I got your message. And my answer is you won't have much longer to wait. I'm coming after you."

"No, you don't get it. I'm coming for you. I haven't seen DeFuniak Springs for some time. I miss it. I'm sure Rocky Steel won't be too hard to find."

"You stay away from Rocky. You've got no business with her."

"Ah, so you like her. Are you fucking her? Of course you are. She's so hot."

"You demented bitch."

"For that, I'm going to do her first. I might even let you watch."

"You fucking psycho. You won't get near Rocky," he said, but the line was dead.

The doctor appeared and walked straight over to L.T. "Your dog will be fine, Mr. Stafford. He's sedated now. Why don't you leave him a day or two? He could use the rest."

"Take good care of him, doc. He's a hero."

"Do what?"

"He helped take down the Interstate Rapist."

"Do tell."

"It's true. He rescued a woman from that killer two weeks ago, saved her life. That's how he got the chest wound. Saved her again this morning. Clamped onto that psycho's arm and wouldn't let go, even though he'd been stabbed again. Held him until we got him."

"Amazing. In that case, he can stay as long as he wants."

147

"Oh, he won't want to stay long. He knows he has a job to do."

"He's a police dog?"

"No, just a very dedicated bodyguard. Give him whatever he needs. I'll stop by tomorrow."

He was out the door and heading for Pensacola. On the way he grabbed a take-out coffee and sipped it in the Blazer. His shoulders slumped; his arms felt weak as lack of sleep began to wear on him. When he reached the hospital, he found it surrounded by television news crews. Walking past them he stopped at the reception desk and said, "I'm here to see Roxanne Steel."

"You with the press?"

"No, ma'am."

"Your name, please?"

"L.T. Stafford."

She checked the list. "Your identification, sir?"

He showed her his driver's license.

"Room 204, sir. You'll need to show your ID before security will let you see her."

He nodded. "Thanks."

She was sleeping when he entered the room. He slid a chair over next to her bed, flopped in it and stretched out his legs. In minutes he dozed off.

"I'd know that snore anywhere," said Rocky.

"Hmm? Shit. I guess I nodded off. How you doing?"

"Oh, I'm fine. Just need a little sleep is all. Did you come to take me home?"

"No, you might as well stay and rest a day or two. Your place is a crime scene. We can't go near it until the investigators finish with it."

"Ah, what the hell. You're probably a lousy cook anyway."

"Glad to see you're okay."

"Likewise. Your chest okay?"

"Feels like somebody parked a truck on it. I'm fine. Beau's fine too. He's with a vet in Fort Walton Beach."

148

"That's really sweet of you, L.T. What are you going to do now? Get a room?"

"Yes. And if you don't mind me using your Blazer I'd like to go down to Ocala and meet with Detective Tom Hardman of the Florida Highway Patrol. He wants to know what I know about the Iceman Killer. And I need to know what he knows."

"I guess I don't mind. Are you coming back?"

"You know it."

"That's good enough for me."

CHAPTER FORTY-ONE

Carla finished offloading in Detroit. Heading south on I-75 with an empty trailer the Kenworth accelerated crisply, reaching the speed limit in no time. Without a pickup order she made for the Detroiter Truck Stop to look for a load, maybe hang out until she found one. But things were beginning to eat away at her. Now he knew who she was and what she wanted. Cops could be looking for her already. Marlin's cup began to jiggle and rattle.

"What do you want?" She looked at the makeshift burial urn. "I know. I fucked up, okay?" It continued to rattle and shake. "Any suggestions smartass?" *What would he do?* she thought. "What would you do, Fish?"

"You're driving a fucking banana. A banana-yellow truck," he would say. She could almost hear his voice. "You stick out like a dog's dick."

"Fine, what am I supposed to do about it?" Her eyes moved back and forth between the road ahead and Marlin's rattling cup. She caught sight of a billboard advertisement for a paint shop. "We paint trucks," she read. "Yeah," she said to the cup. "Yeah, I like that, Fish. But we're not exactly going to make ourselves inconspicuous. We'll just change our identity. Add a little camouflage."

She went on to the truck stop, dropped her trailer, then drove to the paint shop. Inside she found a stout man in blue coveralls and mechanic's skullcap. He was covered in sanding dust from

150

head to toe, including eyebrows, mustache, even the fine hairs on his cheek that escaped the razor were made to look white.

"What can I do for you, Blondie?" he asked with a smile.

"Y'all do custom work?"

"You want it, we do it. What you driving?"

"Longnose Kenworth. A W900."

"Let's go take a look at it," he said, stepping past her to hold the door open for her. Outside he looked over the gleaming yellow truck. "You drive this all by yourself?"

"You want to paint it or are you applying for a job?"

"Okay. None of my business. What you want? Flames? Stripes? A mural? What?"

"Complete color change. Something patriotic. Make it look like the flag."

"Ah, a true American. Driving the Stars and Stripes. The lady has balls, so to speak."

"Can you do it or not?"

"Hell yes, we can do it."

"I mean now."

"Well, now that's another story." He rubbed his chin and looked around the yard. "Got that Volvo that jackknifed, a Western Star needs to be chopped and lowered, and a couple International conventionals for color change. Yours I need five days and seventy-five hundred bucks."

Carla took a deep breath, thrust out her chest until her breasts strained against her sweater and said, "Here's what you do. Three days, six grand."

He chuckled. "Lady," he said between laughs. "You'd have to eat my shorts for that."

"Okay," she said, staring at him without blinking, without expression.

"You're serious?"

"Just get it done."

"Step into my office," he said.

"Step into the shower first, Biff."

"I mean to sign the work order."

"One more thing," said Carla. "I need a loaner car."

"I don't have no loaners."

"What do you drive?"

"That old Dodge pickup."

"It'll do."

He shook his head. "The things a man has to do to get a fuckin' blowjob." He tugged the door open and shouted, "Emil. Get your ass out here and start prepping the KW. It's a rush job."

The next afternoon L.T reported to the Florida Highway Patrol post in Ocala. The duty officer summoned Detective Hardman. Two men in business suits appeared shortly.

"Mr. Stafford, how do you do? I'm Tom Hardman, this is Agent Pedro Costa from the Tampa Field Office of the FBI."

"It's L.T.," he said, shaking hands.

"Call me Tom, L.T. Come right on in. We'll find us a place to chat."

The detective led the way into an interview room. On the table sat a single file folder. Hardman pulled a chair from under the table and motioned for L.T. to sit, then took the chair opposite. Costa sat beside L.T. Opening the folder he passed a neck-up photograph of the victim to L.T. "Do you know this man?"

L.T. shook his head.

"His name is Melvin Flatt. Truck driver from South Bay." He handed over various photos of the frozen victim, the crime scene, and the Crafters number seven screwdriver with L.T.'s name carved into the handle. "What's your connection to all this?"

"Last September a friend asked me to look into the disappearance of her brother, Arnold Perkins. He's the trucker found stabbed to death at the Wildwood Truck Stop. The weapon was a screwdriver just like this one." He pointed to the picture.

"Go on," said Hardman.

"I'm sure you know the rest. Marlin Sears kidnapped my daughter. I freed her from his refrigerated trailer and chased him until he ran into the side of a bridge. He was driving the tractor-trailer rig he stole from Arnold Perkins the night Perkins was murdered."

"How does that connect you to this latest victim?" asked Costa.

"Ever since the previous frozen victim was found two days after Sears died, I haven't been able to bring myself to believe that he was the Iceman Killer. I think that murder and this one were both committed to send the message that the Iceman Killer's still out there, and still operating."

"You indicated you think you know the identity of this killer," said Hardman.

"Oh, I have no doubt as to the identity of the Iceman Killer."

"Well? Who is it?" asked Costa.

"It's Carla Sears. Sister of Marlin. Two weeks ago, she came to Ohio to kill me."

"Okay, she wants revenge at your expense," said Hardman. "But I don't see a motive in the Melvin Flatt killing."

"Believe me she has a motive. She wants to keep me on her tail until I get close enough for her to get another shot at me. She's drawing me into the game. It's tag and I'm it."

"This guy had sex shortly before he died. We got DNA samples and it wasn't his wife," Costa pointed out.

L.T. leaned toward Hardman. "She calls herself Black Widow. It's her CB handle."

"Are you saying she fucked his brains out?" said Hardman. "Then froze him solid?" He shook his head. "She's a psycho."

"She's not crazy," said L.T. "She's cold and calculating. A female Ted Bundy. She knows exactly what she's doing."

"You have any idea what she looks like?" asked Costa.

"I know someone who does."

CHAPTER FORTY-TWO

In the shower at her hotel room near Detroit Carla rubbed in hair dye to change her short, blonde locks to a mousy reddish-brown. After toweling she stood in front of the mirror. "I don't know about this," she said to her reflection. "Could make it damn difficult to get laid." She cupped her breasts, hefting them a bit, feeling their weight in her hands. "Naw," she said and proceeded to dress.

When she arrived at the body shop her star-spangled Kenworth was already sitting out front. Carla laughed out loud as she parked the pickup truck. The stylish, rolling version of the flag brought a smile to her face. Pearl-white stars on a navy background covered most of the hood; red and white stripes adorned much of the rest of the tractor and sleeper. Each side of the hood was also overlaid with an airbrushed screaming eagle, a true symbol of American patriotism. All windows were tinted black, making them all but opaque. She ran her fingers lightly over a fender, feeling the glassy-smooth clear-coat finish, knowing that no one would ever suspect this truck to be driven by anyone but a hardcore patriot, probably a war veteran. Her new disguise lifted the weight of an engine block from her shoulders. She took a breath, the feeling of newfound freedom totally overwhelming her.

A voice from somewhere behind said, "I see you like it." He wiped his hands on a rag, fished some business cards from a pocket in his coveralls and handed them to her. "Tell your friends."

She kept smiling and pulled an envelope from her hip pocket. "Six grand," she said. "It's all there."

He peered into the envelope fanning the bills with a thumb. "What about the rest?" he asked, giving her a wink.

"What rest? Six grand. We agreed."

"Yeah, I know, six grand. What about the little promise you made?"

She was still smiling. "What? What little promise?"

"You know," he said, stepping closer and lowering his voice. "A blowjob?"

Carla stepped back; her smile gone. "Excuse me? This is harassment, isn't it? This is sexual harassment. You're harassing me. A woman comes in paying cash and it's not good enough. You have to pressure her for sex. I bet the police would love to hear about this."

He grabbed his business cards from her, held his hands up and said, "Okay, lady. Have a nice life." He turned and disappeared into the shop, shaking his head and muttering as he walked through the door.

Carla chuckled as she fired up the Kenworth and headed for the Detroiter Truck Stop to retrieve her trailer on her way to Willard, Ohio to pick up a load of riding lawnmowers going to Tampa. From there the plan was to run east on State Route 60 to Vero Beach. But she wouldn't go home. She would leave the truck and trailer at the truck stop as usual, hop into her Sierra pickup and head for DeFuniak Springs on a mission. News reports of the death of the Interstate Rapist told her where to look for L.T. Stafford and Roxanne Steel.

Rocky sat on the side of the hospital bed, dressed and ready to go when he arrived. "Hey, truck driver," she said.

"You ready to head for home?"

"Head for the house, we call it."

"Guess I'm not really a truck driver."

"We'll get you there," she said. "Now get me out of here."

They were barely on the road to Rocky's house when L.T.'s cell phone rang. He tugged it from the holster and handed it across to Rocky.

"Hello," she said.

"Hello," said a woman. "Who's this?"

"This is Rocky."

"Rocky? Did you say Rocky?"

"Yes. Rocky. Who's this?"

"Well, if that ain't a coincidence. I just met a Rocky the other day in Vero Beach."

The hairs on Rocky's nape began to tingle and crawl upward. Her hands trembled. "Black Widow? Carla?"

"The one and the same, Honey. How's your sweet lips?"

L.T. waved at her to give him the phone, but she held it to her ear. He switched on the right turn signal and eased off the gas pedal.

"What do you want?" asked Rocky.

"I was looking for L.T. Stafford. You wouldn't happen to know him, would you? About six-foot, graying, cold-blooded killer."

"He...he's busy right now."

"Tell him to un-busy himself. He can talk to me."

L.T. stopped the Blazer on the shoulder. Taking the phone from her he said, "This is L.T."

"Well, if it isn't the famous killer."

"What do you want?"

"I want you. Dead."

"Why?"

"Don't fuck with me. You know what I'm talking about."

"Okay. But you screwed up, didn't you? You only wounded me. Is that the best you can do?"

She screamed. "Why aren't you home, you son of a bitch?"

"Why? Where are you?"

"Fourteen-twenty River Road, White Falls, Ohio."

L.T. hung up and called Chet's cell phone. It went to voice mail. He hung up and called White Falls Police. Sharon Thompson, dispatcher and niece of Mayor Louis Thompson answered the phone.

"White Falls Police Department."

"Sharon, this is L.T."

"Well, Chief, what can I do for you?" she asked.

"Sharon, get somebody over to my place right away. The real Iceman Killer is there now."

"Don't be ridiculous. The Iceman Killer is dead."

"Just do it."

"Okay, I'm on it." She hung up.

L.T. punched in his home number. His answering machine took the call. "L.T.'s house. Sorry, the rat bastard isn't home. But I see he knows some famous people. Leave a message. I'll pass it on. I promise."

He hung up and called Chet's cell phone again, leaving a message.

Rocky stared at him, terror evident in her eyes. "What the hell was that all about?"

"Black Widow just upped the stakes."

"I'm afraid to ask what you mean."

"She found out my daughter is Cheryl Dakota."

"Cheryl Dakota? The singer? Come on." She could tell from his expression he meant it. "No shit? Cheryl Dakota is really your daughter?"

He nodded.

"That means," she took a moment to think about it. "You were married to Nat Pearce."

"Not exactly. We were high school sweethearts. I joined the Marines, shipped out not knowing she was pregnant. I only recently found out about Cheryl when she showed up at my door."

"Damn," she said. "That is a sad story. But at least it has a happy ending."

"Not yet," he said. "It's not over yet. Now this crazy woman knows my family. Knows I know you. No one is safe as long as she's out there."

"What are we going to do?"

"I don't know yet. But I'd better call Cheryl." He punched in her number. She answered on the third ring. "Hello."

"Cheryl, thank God you're all right. Are you home?"

"That's a hell of a greeting. Since when did you find God?"

He filled her in. She told him not to worry, that she and her mother have a good security team and that he should know that. But he wasn't satisfied.

"Tell the security people to keep an eye out for her. She's crazy and will stop at nothing to hurt me in whatever way she can. That puts you and your mother in great danger."

"I'll tell them right away. You be careful. You hear me?"

"I do this for a living. Remember?"

"I remember seeing you in the hospital with a hole in your chest."

"Are you going to keep throwing that in my face?"

She chuckled. "Just watch your back. I love you, Dad."

"Love you too, Sweetie." He hung up.

Rocky's jaw gaped. "That was really her. That was Cheryl Dakota. She's got the voice of an angel, just like Nat."

L.T. beamed with pride. "You like country music?"

"Only the good stuff. And those two are the best."

L.T. put his phone away. Checking the mirror, he eased the Blazer back onto the roadway. The car grew quiet as the driver and passenger struggled with the question of how to avoid the dangers facing them.

CHAPTER FORTY-THREE

L.T. and Rocky drove to Fort Walton Beach on the way to her house. When they reached the clinic, the parking lot was jammed with cars. L.T. found a spot on the street and they walked in to find the waiting area crammed with people. At the center of it all stood Beau, taking pats on the back. He spotted Rocky and gave a sharp bark. The crowd backed off giving him room to prance. Rocky pushed her way through the group. Beau sidled up to her and wagged his bobtail.

"He's a celebrity," said the receptionist over the noise of the people filling the room. "He caught the Interstate Rapist."

"I know," Rocky replied. "He saved my life. Twice."

The crowd cheered.

"You must be Ms. Steel."

"That's right. How is my hero?"

"Oh, he's fine. The doctor stitched up his head wound and checked him all over. He's in very good shape, considering."

"Have you got my bill ready?"

"Oh, there's no bill. He's the greatest hero we've ever seen. The doctor says any animal does that much for the community stays here for free. Besides, we've never seen so many people around here. They've been lining up for two days. We couldn't buy advertising this good."

"Well, thank you. That's very kind. Please convey my heartfelt gratitude to the doctor."

"I surely will, ma'am. Y'all take care now. Bye, Beau."

Rocky hooked the lead to Beau's collar. The crowd parted to allow them to make their exit, cheering again.

"You're just eating this up, Beau Steel," she said to him as they walked toward the Blazer. Even L.T. had to reach down to stroke the dog's back in appreciation.

L.T. got Rocky and Beau settled in at her house, the crime scene finally released and they enjoyed a couple days together, then he headed back to Ocala to talk strategy with Detective Hardman and FBI agent Costa. Unfortunately, it turned out to be all Florida strategy and nothing to do with the rest of the country where he and Rocky, would not necessarily be encountering trouble from Black Widow, who was able to strike from anywhere in the country.

Three days later Carla parked her Sierra across from the United States Post Office in DeFuniak Springs, Florida. Her watch said four-twenty. She pulled the beer can from the cup holder and sipped at it. After twenty minutes or so a handful of workers began to exit the building. Her eyes followed a tanned young man with tousled brown hair as he climbed into a dark blue pickup truck with tinted windows. In a moment she was following him as he made his way out of town. Before long the pickup began to slow. Its right turn indicator flashed.

"Perfect," said Carla as the truck swung into the parking lot of Red's Country Tavern. Carla pulled in and parked beside him. Only two other cars sat in the lot.

"Man," said the young man. "You made a wrong turn. Interstate's back that way." He pointed, smiling.

"They got cold beer in there?"

"I reckon they do."

"Then I'm in the right place."

"There you go."

"Your turn to buy, isn't it?"

"Do I know you, Angel, or am I sleepin' on the job again and dreamin'?"

"Tell you what. Let's get a beer and you can pinch me, see if it's a dream."

"Now you're talkin'." He pulled the door open, holding it for her.

CHAPTER FORTY-FOUR

Carla whipped off her sunglasses as she entered the dimly lit bar. The smell of stale beer mingled with the odors of urine and sweat raised up to slap her in the face. She cursed as she bumped into a table, her hands groping in the darkness. A strong hand clamped about her bicep, steadying her, then led her to a seat at a table in the corner.

"Now there's a sight ya don't see every day," called the bartender. "Bobby Maxwell with a woman. And she looks human, too."

"You got a real way with words, Red. Why don't you take your head outta your ass and bring us a couple beers?"

"What? No champagne?"

The young man glared back at him. The bartender pulled two beers, set them on a tray and carried them over as the couple sat down. He put the drinks in front of them and returned to the bar without another word.

"Bobby Maxwell," said the young man, extending a meaty paw.

Carla took it and said, "Rosie."

"How do, Rosie. What brings you to the springs?"

"Business."

He nodded, smiling and watching her breasts strain against her tank top with each breath. "So, what kind of business you in?"

"Long-haul trucking. Perishable goods mostly. You know, fruits and vegetables."

"No shit. You drive an eighteen-wheeler?"

162

"Sure do."

"What a coincidence. For the first time in my life, I have this uncontrollable urge to make love to a trucker."

"Sounds serious," she said, smiling. "How long have you known you were gay?"

Bobby burst into laughter, spitting beer and coughing. When he got his breath he said, "Y'all know what I'm talkin' about."

"What business are you in, Bobby?"

"Kinda the same as you, Rosie." He leaned over, looked at her cleavage and said, "I deliver."

"I'm happy to hear it."

"Me too, 'cause I got a major load for you."

"Just what is it you deliver?"

"The U.S. Mail, darlin'."

"Get outta town."

He nodded, swigging his beer.

"Then maybe you're just the person I need to talk to."

"I knew I was. I could tell I was just the right man for you."

"You work for the Post Office, right?"

He nodded again.

"Well, my business up here is very serious. I'm looking for the bitch that's been stealing my business and slandering my good name. I built my business on my reputation for always coming… uh, coming through, I mean. And I can't let her ruin me. I've got to find her and tell her in no uncertain terms to lay off."

"I reckon I can help you, all right. If she gets mail through my depot, I know where to find her."

"She goes by the name of Rocky. Roxanne Steel is her name." She saw his eyes widen. "You, by any chance, know her?"

He shrugged. "I might."

"So? You gonna tell me?"

"Not yet."

"What the fuck do you mean, not yet?"

"I work for the United States Government. I'm not allowed to give out confidential information. Besides, I might be country, but I ain't stupid. I tell you now, you're outta here. I'm left sittin' with a big dick in my hand."

"Hope it's yours."

"Wanna find out?"

"Will it get me to Roxanne Steel?"

"Guaranteed."

"Let's do it."

They finished their beers and headed out the door. Carla followed his pickup to a rundown trailer on a wooded lot just off the main road. A large, black Labrador lay chained to a homemade doghouse near the front door. He never moved as they walked past. A beagle began to bay from somewhere inside. Bobby tugged the door open and yelled, "Go lay down Rufus or you'll get no supper."

Carla tiptoed in behind him. He walked straight to the refrigerator and pulled two beers. He walked back, handed her a beer and kissed her on the mouth. Sitting down on the couch he tugged her into his lap. With one hand on his beer, the other on a breast he locked his lips on hers again. Despite the overall squalor of the surroundings, she didn't at all mind being groped and mauled in the interest of prosperity. Besides, the place really wasn't much different from the old two-bedroom, clapboard sided house she grew up in just outside Zephyrhills. The ranch, she and Marlin had called it. The place where their father had failed at raising beef cattle, not to mention parenting.

Bobby put his beer on a cluttered end table next to the sofa and tugged her tank top over her head to reveal cream-colored swells that gently curved and made the nipples point slightly upward. He buried his face roughly in their fullness as Carla went for his belt.

A while later they sat together on the sofa, catching their breath and sipping beer.

Overdrive

"Okay," said Carla. "Tell me about Roxanne Steel."

Bobby shrugged. "What do you want to know?"

"Let's start with where she lives."

"That all? Shit, that's easy. I thought you wanted something tough. Like who she gets mail from."

Carla stared at him a moment. "You know, that's not a bad idea. I'll bet you could tell me which outfit she gets her paychecks from."

"Not off the top of my head. But if there's something coming through the system in the morning, I reckon I can."

"When will I know?"

"Meet me down the road from her place about ten in the morning."

"I would if you'd tell me where she lives."

"SR83. Number 17229. I'll look for y'all at the filling station next to the Interstate where 83 crosses it."

She fetched her clothes from the floor and began to slip into them.

"What's your hurry?"

"Work to do. I came a long way to get my business back."

"How about a little special consideration for giving up confidential information?"

"I just fucked your brains out, Bobby. It don't get more special than that. And by the way, how is it you know exactly where she lives?"

"I know where the babes are. Believe me, in these parts there ain't all that many you'd take home before closing time."

Carla shook her head.

"How bad you want this info?"

"Not that bad," she replied.

"Just the same, we're talkin' about me fixin' to commit a federal offence. I reckon I'm gonna have to hold out for another ride."

"Are you gonna be an asshole about this?"

"Nope. But I reckon I'm gonna be a prick."

She pulled her top back off and sat down beside him. "You better have what I want in the morning."

"I got what you want right now," he said, stroking himself.

CHAPTER FORTY-FIVE

Following Maxwell's directions, Carla took a drive past Rocky's house in the early evening just before sundown. The sun dipped behind the pines and turned a few fluffy clouds into orange fireballs dotting the purple sky. She kept her hair hidden under a baseball cap in an attempt to avoid being recognized and rode low in the seat of her pickup, peering out the side window as she passed the bungalow. Lights burned inside. The Peterbilt and Great Dane reefer sat in the driveway. No other vehicle could be seen. "Well, Rocky," she said in the direction of the house. "Your boyfriend in there with you?"

She cruised back into town and stopped at a pay phone. In the directory she located Rocky's home number and jotted it down. A few minutes later she pulled her car onto the grassy shoulder of SR83 a hundred or so yards from Rocky's house. She punched in the number.

"Hello," Rocky answered.

"Hey, Rocky."

There was silence for a long moment.

"It's Carla. Remember me? I bet you do."

"What do you want?"

"I want your boyfriend."

"What are you talking about?"

"I'm talking about L.T. Stafford. The guy you're fucking."

"He's not here."

167

"Sure, he is."

"He had to go away. He's at a meeting with the FBI."

"Oh, of course he is." Carla slammed her arm against the car door. "When's he coming back?"

"I don't know. What do you want him for?"

"You know what I want him for. Tell him to call me. I'm in Detroit waiting for him." She gave the number.

"I know you killed my husband," Rocky blurted.

"Do what now?"

"My husband, Nick Steel. You killed him in Indiana."

"Well, what a small world. Nick. Road Hog. I remember his... handsome face." Carla's shrill laughter reverberated in Rocky's skull. Then without another word the killer hung up.

L.T.'s cell phone rang. "This is L.T."

"Hey, it's Rocky."

"Hey, yourself. How are you?"

"To tell you the truth I'm a bit rattled. Carla just called. She sounded so creepy. She's really got me spooked. Says she's in Detroit waiting for you. She gave me her number there for you to call. I told her I knew she killed my husband. She as much as admitted it. Said she remembered him. Called him Road Hog. That was his CB handle. I'm scared, L.T."

"Well, if Carla's in Detroit you have nothing to fear from her. Besides, it's me she wants." He thought for a moment. "Look, I'll be finished here tomorrow and will haul ass back to your place. Then I'll get a flight back to Ohio and take care of her once and for all."

"I want to go with you. Could we go together?"

"I don't think that's a good idea. You'll be out of danger if you stay home."

"I won't hear of it. I have a score to settle, too. If you won't go with me, I'll go myself."

OVERDRIVE

"Okay, okay. You win. I'll be back tomorrow and we'll talk about what we're going to do."

Later he called Chet Connor's cell phone from his hotel room.

"Hello," Chet answered.

"How are you, Chet? By the way, the reason I called, Carla phoned Rocky tonight. Left a Detroit number for me to call. Could you check it out for me?" He dictated the number.

"Of course. When will you be back?"

"Soon. If Carla's in Detroit."

CHAPTER FORTY-SIX

The next morning Carla sat waiting in her pickup at the gas station just off I-10 at SR83 when Bobby Maxwell appeared out of nowhere and slipped in beside her.

He grinned and said, "Got the goods." His right hand waved a small stack of letters.

She snatched it from him and began to study the return addresses. "Florida Power," she read aloud. "County Tire Sales and Service, here's a fuel bill, credit card bill. Great, Bobby. That's just great. You got dick."

He reached behind him and pulled an envelope from the pocket of his shorts. "Got the real deal right here."

She tried to grab it but he snatched his hand away.

"What's it worth to you?" he asked, still grinning.

"I paid you yesterday. You forget how good it was?"

"No, I ain't forgot. Reckon I just want some more, is all."

"Hand it over." She held out her hand. "You got the best your sorry ass will ever have. If you want to fix it so you never have it again just go ahead and piss me off. Give."

He handed it over.

"Well, well. What do we have here? Looks like a check. From Boston Freight Forwarding in Michigan." She tore it open.

"Hey, you can't do that. That's tampering with the US Mail. That's a federal offence."

"So, what you gonna do, Bobby? You gonna report me? You wanna explain to the cops how you gave me someone else's mail? I think not."

"You can't steal that check, Rosie. We could both go to jail."

"Who's stealing it? I just want the phone number of this Boston outfit." She fished the check from the envelope. A piece of notepaper came out with it. "Hi Rocky," she read aloud. "Sorry about your ordeal. Saw you on the news. Glad to see you're okay. Jimmy Boston." She rolled her eyes. "Ain't that touching?" She wrote the address and phone number on a note pad and gave the mail back to Bobby.

"What the hell am I supposed to do with this?" he asked.

"Deliver it," Carla replied.

When he was gone, she placed a call to Everett Carlisle at the Carlisle Groves and Packing House in Frostproof, Florida.

"Carlisle," a familiar voice answered.

"Hey, Everett. It's Carla."

"Hey yourself, sweetness. I got you down for a pickup tomorrow, just like you asked. Load's going to the Motor City. Get yourself here early. I'll take you to breakfast."

"I'm not going to be able to make it. Sorry, my truck's laid up. But I want you to give the load to my sister. Her name's Rocky Steel. She works through a broker in Michigan called Boston Freight Forwarding. Ever heard of it?"

"Can't say I have. Your sister got good equipment?"

"The very best."

"All right. I'll call this Boston and see if she's available."

"Everett, you gotta insist you get her and nobody else. They'll give the load to some no-account Yankee if you don't."

"The hell they will. Rocky Steel or they don't get my business. You be good, sweetness. If you can't be good, you call me first."

Rocky busied herself with cleanup and repairs to her house, doing whatever she could to remove any trace of Lyle Crowder and the crime scene aftermath of his attack. Her insurance company sent a crew to replace the door and frame Crowder had demolished upon his first visit, as well as the window shattered when Beau leaped through it to save her life. The workmen asked too many questions, having seen the news reports. She did her best to avoid answering them. To her it just wasn't the glamorous death of a media giant at the hands of an underdog, small-town superhero. Her reality was that of a night of brutal carnage and senseless mortality that she dearly wanted to see fade in her rearview mirror. She wished L.T. was there to protect her from her memories.

The ringing phone startled her. "Hello," she answered.

"Hi, Rocky. It's Jimmy. How are you doing? I saw you on CNN. Are you okay?"

"Hey, Boston. Sure, I'm fine."

"Did you get my note? I put it in with your check."

"Hasn't made its way down here yet."

"Should be there any day. How's your dog? He got wounded again I see."

"We're both recovering nicely. Vacation is good for us." She cleared her throat. "Boston, why do I get the feeling you're beating around the bush trying to get up the nerve to ask me something you know you shouldn't ask?"

He chuckled. "As a matter of fact, I do have a favor to ask."

CHAPTER FORTY-SEVEN

L.T. fished out his cell phone and punched in Rocky's number.

"Hello."

"Hey, Rocky. I'm on my way back."

"Great. "I've got our transportation arranged to Detroit."

"How's that?"

"I've got us a straight load of citrus to the Motor City. We can pick it up tomorrow, first thing in the morning. With both of us driving we'll be up there late the next day."

He thought for a moment. "You know, that's not a bad idea. I could use some time at the wheel to sort a few things out."

"Any of them about me?"

"As a matter of fact, I am kind of jealous of Beau."

"Don't be. He's here for protection and companionship. Besides, he can't drive."

"And me?"

"You? Why you're pure recreation. And driving, of course."

"Somewhere in there lies a reason for me to smile," he said. "Wait a second. I thought you were on vacation. What happened?"

"Got a special request from my broker to handle a load for a new customer. Flattery works with me, just in case you're taking notes."

"That happen often? The special request, I mean."

"Not to me. I'm trying to believe it's genuine and not just another scheme designed by Jimmy Boston to keep my ass moving freight and paying his bills. Why?"

"Nothing. Just wondered."

"Just get your butt back here. I miss you. And that hasn't happened to me lately. I can't wait to see what we make of it."

"Me too.

Next morning Rocky gently rode the brakes as the Peterbilt crested the hill and bled off speed rumbling south into the sleepy town of Clermont on US27. A flaming orange sun burst over the treetops on her left, shooting golden spears into the gray-blue morning sky. L.T.'s cell phone rang. "This is L.T.," he answered.

"L.T., it's Chet. Didn't wake you, did I?"

"Me? The cop who never sleeps?"

"Didn't think so. Listen, that number you gave me turned out to be a rented room at the Detroiter Truck Stop. Registered in the name of Carla Sears. I ran over last night to have a look. Nobody's been sleeping in her bed, including her. The phone is forwarded to a remote, probably a cell phone. She could be anywhere."

"Why doesn't that surprise me? And why does she want me to think she's in Detroit?"

"Yeah. Assuming that to kill you, she'll have to get the drop on you, why doesn't she want you in her neck of the woods? Familiar territory. Why up here?"

"Who knows? Maybe she's just being cocky. Maybe she wants me to know she's good enough to get me anywhere."

"I don't know. From what you've told me about her I have to think she's more cunning than cocky."

"Maybe she *is* setting me up on her territory. Maybe she figures I'll drop my guard while I'm down here thinking she's up there. Maybe she's watching me right now."

"Watch your back, my friend." Chet hung up.

"Trouble?" asked Rocky.

"Could be. Keep your eyes peeled for Carla's truck. Shouldn't be hard to spot. It looks almost the same as this one."

"I thought she was in Detroit."

"So did I."

CHAPTER FORTY-EIGHT

An hour later Rocky backed the Great Dane gently against the loading dock at Carlisle's in Frostproof. A graying, suntanned gentleman in Polo shirt and khaki slacks met them as they topped the steps to the dock. "How do, ma'am. You must be Rocky," he said, his right hand extended.

"I am, sir. Are you Mr. Carlisle?" Rocky shook his hand briefly, keeping it business-like.

"Call me Everett. And this is?"

"L.T. Stafford. Call me L.T." They shook hands.

"Thank you, L.T. I don't mean to pry, but what's the arrangement here? I mean, which one of you am I doing business with? Do you both work for Boston?"

"I'm independent," Rocky replied. "Boston finds me loads. L.T. drives for me."

"Ah," said Everett. "Well, I have a straight load of grapefruit to Detroit. Can you make it by two o'clock tomorrow afternoon?"

"Lucky we're running team this week. That's thirty hours and counting," said Rocky. "How fast can you get us out of here?"

"We'll slip-sheet it on in thirty minutes. Paperwork's all set. Just need you to sign."

Rocky looked at her watch. "How heavy is it?"

"Run you about forty-eight thousand."

176

Rocky winced. "Damn, that's a load. We'll have to run light on fuel and we'll still fracture a law or two. Tell me something, Everett. What happens if we don't make it on time?"

"Oh, you'll still get paid, if that's what you're worried about. But I won't be impressed with you or Boston. After all, I'm told you're the best they have."

"That's mostly because I'm the safest." *Heavy and no time,* she thought. *The kind of run that makes a safe driver reckless.* She felt like telling him to shove it.

"Rocky," he said smiling. "How dangerous is a grapefruit?" He walked over to a stack of cartons, opened one and lobbed her a sample. "If you make it, you and Boston will get a lot of business from me. And I'm not one to haggle over freight rates."

It's not the grapefruit I'm worried about. It's the fruitcakes on the highway between here and the Motor City. She sighed. "All right, Everett. We'll be in Detroit tomorrow at two. That is, we'll damn sure try."

He motioned to a forklift driver and the machine lurched forward. Thirty minutes later L.T. closed the doors on the trailer and fired up the reefer unit as Rocky came down the steps with the bill of lading.

Carlisle walked to the edge of the dock. "Y'all have a safe trip now. Tell your sister I said hello."

"My sister?" Rocky and L.T. both looked puzzled.

"Carla and I are old friends. She recommended you. Funny. I never knew she had a sister."

"Carla's not-." L.T. clutched her arm and squeezed. "When did you see her, Everett?"

"Ain't seen her lately. She called me from Detroit a couple days ago to arrange this pickup."

"Tell her we said hello," L.T. said

"Sure enough," said Everett, turning to walk back to his office.

"What the hell is going on?" asked Rocky.

"Let the games begin," said L.T. "Looks like Carla set us up."

"For what?"

"I expect we'll find out soon enough."

They settled into the cab. Rocky fired the Caterpillar and let it idle. "We're running right on maximum gross weight, maybe even a little over so here's what we do. We'll go to a truck stop scale to check individual axle weights, adjust the fifth wheel and trailer tandems to get as close to legal as we can. We don't take on any fuel until we're past the Florida scales. Then we take on just enough to get us beyond the next weigh station. We'll have to do that all the way up."

"Is fuel that heavy?"

"Twenty-four hundred pounds, full up. Keeping the fuel supply low will shed some weight and could mean the difference between a diesel bear writing us up or looking the other way. It's going to make for some time wasted on fuel stops. So, I'll take the first shift. Then you'll have to run full hours to keep me legal in that department." She shook her head. "No, that's not going to work. That will put you behind the wheel in the mountains in the middle of the night with a heavy load. On second thought, you better take the wheel now. Later, I'll try to get some sleep so I can run through the nightshift."

"You know," L.T. said, "The man in me wants to say you don't trust me. But the wise man in me knows enough to say thanks."

"You didn't have to say that; but I'm glad you did. This load, this deadline and now that killer bitch after us." She shook her head. "Think my normally good judgment blew a tire today."

L.T. smiled, climbed out and went around to the driver's seat as Rocky switched places.

"Keep an eye on that air gauge," said Rocky. "The pressure doesn't seem to be coming up as quickly as usual."

He nodded, depressing the accelerator a little to bring up the revs. "Seems to be rising now," he said, as the engine speed drove the air compressor faster.

OVERDRIVE

"Okay. Just keep an eye on it. We're going to need all the braking power we've got."

He rested a hand on the shifter, ready to slip it into gear and get underway.

"Wait,' said Rocky. She leaned over and kissed him gently on the lips. He let go the stick and pulled her close. After a moment their lips parted and he released her.

"Whew," she gasped. "Any more of that and we kiss our deadline goodbye. But I needed it. I mean, it's good to know I'm not in shit this deep on my own." She rolled her eyes. "That probably didn't come out quite right."

L.T. smiled. Shortly they were rolling out of the loading area approaching US27. He depressed the brake pedal before entering the highway but under even a small amount of momentum the weight of the load wanted to keep the rig rolling. When the truck didn't slow quickly enough, he stepped harder on the treadle. The rig suddenly shuddered to an abrupt stop almost pitching Rocky from her seat. Beau sprang up and dug his claws into the carpet to keep from sliding.

"Good," Rocky said, smiling. "We've got that one out of our system. Now, just try to relax and ease it up the road. You'll get the feel of it as you go. Remember not to get close to anyone. You need lots of stopping distance now."

L.T. smirked, swinging the rig out onto the highway, checking the mirrors to watch the trailer clear the turn and line itself up neatly behind the Peterbilt. When he reached a comfortable cruising speed, he tugged his phone from its holster and passed it to Rocky. "Time to find out if Doobie's in the neighborhood. This late in the week he's usually picking up a load to head back up north. Maybe we'll get lucky. Press Menu. The number's in memory."

"Calling in reinforcements?"

"We can use all the help we can get."

179

When Doobie didn't answer she left a message, then asked, "Shouldn't we call the State Police? Or maybe even that FBI guy, Agent Costa?"

"I'm afraid we don't really have any proof that Carla's in the area. Or that she actually committed the crimes we believe she did. I don't think we could expect much more than a big delay while we try to explain this mess."

"We can't afford that. I don't want Boston to start holding up my freight checks. If we screw this up the son of a bitch will do that. For certain."

"I can have a little pressure exerted on him to speed things up if need be."

"No, you don't get it. If I don't bring this load in on time that fat prick will take it personally. He'll see that my reputation implodes. He can do that. He knows everyone in this business. I'll end up sitting in truck stops waiting for loads of turnips."

L.T. cleared his throat. "I got it," he said. He swung the rig into the left lane to give clearance to a tractor-trailer sitting on the narrow shoulder.

Rocky reached over and plucked the CB mike from its ceiling mount. "Eighteen on the side, you okay?"

No answer.

"Eighteen-wheeler on the side, you need help?" she called again.

Still no reply.

"Man," said L.T. "You see the paint job on that rig?"

Rocky whistled. "Pretty fancy. All stars and stripes with a big eagle. Don't know if I'd want to be down here making a statement like that."

"What? That you're a proud American?"

"No, that I'm an obnoxious Yankee and well south of the Ohio River."

"Ah," L.T. said, nodding. "Obviously a northerner."

"Guess he doesn't need help. Let's get up the road."

180

CHAPTER FORTY-NINE

L.T. depressed the accelerator a little more. The engine roared. Slowly the speedometer needle crept upward a bit as the engine labored under its heavy load. It seemed like he had just reached cruising speed when he backed off to slow the rig as they approached traffic lights at the junction of Interstate 4 near Haines City. When the light turned amber, he eased down on the brake treadle. Something made a loud pop followed by a hiss from the rush of pressurized air escaping. The needle on the air gauge dropped to zero. Emergency spring brakes applied suddenly, pitching Rocky forward. She jammed her palms against the dash as the rig shuddered to a stop, its engine dead. Beau slid forward and barked sharply when he rammed the gear stick.

"What the hell just happened?" L.T. cried.

"Blew an airline," said Rocky, calmly. "Switch on the emergency flashers, then come out and direct traffic while I go below and take a look." She climbed down, sat on the pavement and slid herself under the tractor just ahead of the drive axles. "There's a tool kit in the compartment under the sleeper on the right side," she called out. "Hand me down the adjustable wrench."

He fished through the toolbox until he found it and passed it down to her. Horns honked incessantly as two lanes of traffic jammed into single file to get past. Several drivers offered one-finger salutes. Others verbally expressed their feelings for truckers.

Five minutes later Rocky emerged, a spot of black grease smeared on her forehead.

"Okay," she said. "We can go now."

L.T.'s mouth still hung open as he climbed behind the wheel. Rocky stowed the wrench and joined him.

"Build up the pressure and we're on our way," said Rocky. She looked at her reflection in the visor mirror and dabbed at the grease spot with a tissue.

"You fixed it? Already?"

"Don't look so surprised. What? You thought that I was only good in bed?"

He grinned. "That too. What was it?"

"Sabotage."

"Seriously?"

"Dead serious. Wrench marks on the main airline where it supplies the tanks. Vibration from the engine and the road shook it until it came apart. We're damn lucky it happened now. We could have killed someone. Like us. Dead."

"So, someone loosened the air line, knowing it would eventually come apart and very likely cause an accident. When could that have been done?"

"Had to be while we were loading."

L.T. nodded. "She's very close. Probably watching us right now." He gazed around.

A W900 Kenworth with patriotic paint scheme, black tinted windows and a stainless-steel Great Dane trailer slipped past them.

"Guess that guy didn't need help after all," said L.T. The air pressure rose quickly. In minutes they were ready to roll on. L.T. eased the rig into the Haines City Truck Stop where they scaled and adjusted axle weights.

CHAPTER FIFTY

They were just nicely back on the highway when the cell phone rang. "Hello," Rocky answered.

"Bonjour, L.T. Your voice is changing. Must be your shorts too tight, eh," he kidded.

"Hey, Doobie. It's Rocky. L.T. has his hands full. He's behind the wheel."

"How are you, Rocky? You stole my best driver, eh?"

"He saved my life. I figured the least I could do was keep him off the streets."

"You didn't fall for that hero shit, did you? He's always pulling that just to get attention from pretty girls."

"Where are you, Doobie?"

"Just finished loading tomatoes in Ruskin. Getting my shit together for a run to Toronto. What you need?"

"We're a bit ahead of you. We're on US27 just north of Haines City on our way to Detroit. Carla Sears is in the neighborhood and she's out to get us. She already tried once. We could really use an extra pair of eyes watching our back door."

"Tell Super Cop I've got him covered. Meet you at the truck stop in Wildwood."

"Can't do it. We've got to dodge the scale at Belleview. We're a little heavy with the fuel we're carrying."

"Okay, I'll look for you above Ocala. Call me when you're on the big road." He hung up.

183

Doobie caught up with them near Gainesville at noon. They agreed to communicate by cell phone to avoid CB conversation that could easily be picked up by Carla. Doobie stayed behind a couple hundred yards as they worked their way north. There were no more mysterious incidents that afternoon and not a single sighting of Carla or her yellow Kenworth. With things remaining quiet Rocky managed to catch a few hours in the sleeper getting ready for her long nightshift.

L.T., though silent most of the day, maintained a vigilant watch from the driver's seat of the Peterbilt. Gradually he gained confidence in his driving ability as he practiced braking the heavy load for weigh stations and short fuel stops. By seven in the evening, they neared Atlanta. L.T. took the Forest Park exit, needing a break and a bite to eat before heading into the taller hills to the north. Doobie followed, parking a few spots away at the truck stop. If Carla was dogging L.T., it made sense to keep Doobie's presence a surprise to her. Let her find out the hard way that L.T. had help. Although he wasn't sure what aid Doobie could render in a confrontation, he felt somewhat better knowing he was there. But what he really wanted to know was what Carla was doing, and where.

They rolled past Chattanooga at ten-thirty, still on schedule to make Detroit on time. Rocky emerged from the sleeper, flopping into the passenger seat.

"Get any sleep?" asked L.T.

"A bit," she replied. "It's so creepy. I can't help thinking she's watching us."

"Oh, I'm sure she is. Look at this maze of traffic. Cars and trucks everywhere. She could be in any one of them, setting us up for God knows what."

"You think she's in a car?"

"I don't know. But I wouldn't rule it out as a means of surprising us, spying on us without arousing suspicion. I've been watching the traffic, mentally trying to recognize which vehicles seem to

OVERDRIVE

hang around us, could be watching us. There are a few cars. A white Lincoln, couple Chevs and a Ford pickup. Can't really tell who's driving them but they keep showing up in our vicinity."

"Any trucks?"

"Just one that makes me nervous," he said. "The one with the fancy paint job and black windows. The obnoxious Yankee."

"Or the well-disguised unstable serial killer bitch. Where is it now?"

He glanced in the left mirror. "Right behind us."

Rocky peered at the reflection in the right mirror. "Take the Cleveland exit just up the road. Let's go into the truck stop. See what happens. It's time for me to take over anyway."

CHAPTER FIFTY-ONE

L.T. signaled a right turn as they approached the exit. He let out a long, slow breath as the Kenworth pulled into the left lane, passed them and motored on. He wheeled the Peterbilt into a parking spot near the restaurant at Cleveland, Tennessee. Rocky took Beau for a walk while L.T. picked up a couple of take-out coffees and a bottle of water for the dog. Shortly, they rolled on up I-75 north toward Knoxville with Rocky behind the wheel.

L.T. marveled at how Rocky always seemed to be all business behind the wheel. Her eyes or hands or feet or some combination of the three was constantly in motion, working and monitoring while pulling a load just a shade over the legal limit. Later, as they crawled up the steep grade into the Smokys just above Knoxville, she took a second to look over at L.T. and said, "By the way, nice work." She flashed him a smile that glowed in the dim light from the instruments. "You covered a lot of highway under pressure. You got the job done. You did well."

He nodded to her, then stared out into the darkness, unable to stop smiling himself. He liked this woman. The way she never seemed to judge him, just went about her business. The way she looked. The way she made him feel so young and virile and excited about being alive.

As they crested the climb and began to pick up speed running along the "top of the rock" where I-75 bridges the peaks of the range, a familiar voice crackled over the CB. It was their French-Canadian friend.

"L.T. I mean Peacemaker. It's me, eh. Doobie."

After a moment L.T. answered. "I thought we weren't going to use the radio."

"It's a little late for that, monsieur. You know that KW with the flag all over it that's been following us?"

"Yeah, what about it?"

"It just drew alongside me and tooted the air horn."

"So?"

"So, when it pulled in front of me, I noticed the name on the back door of the reefer. It's Black Widow."

Rocky's arms went rigid, her knuckles whitened on the wheel.

The hair stood up on the back of L.T.'s neck.

"Looks like she's going to pass us," said Rocky, her eyes fixed on the mirror, watching the lights of the Kenworth grow larger as it approached.

"Or something," L.T. added.

"Yeah, that's what I meant."

"Isn't that long, steep downhill grade up ahead here somewhere?"

"Jellico," Rocky replied, nodding. "It's just ahead. And it's a long way down. What's that tell you?"

"She's about to make her move," said L.T. "I've only seen that rock a couple of times but that's enough to know it's a nasty place to get a load like this separated from the roadway."

Rocky nodded. "She knows we're loaded to the ass and will be using all the brakes we've got just to keep us upright flying through the curves on that mountain."

"She set us up with a super-heavy load and a tight schedule so she could have us right where she wants us. Man, we walked into this with blinders on."

"I'm sorry, L.T.," said Rocky. "I never should have taken this load."

187

"Not your fault. You were just doing your job. I was wrong to get you involved in this."

"Hey, let's not forget I paid my dues, too. That crazy bitch killed my husband. You're not the only one with a score to settle."

He nodded. Rocky lifted her foot off the accelerator as they crested the final peak and rolled into the long, steep downgrade that led into Kentucky at the bottom, four miles ahead. The highway fell away before them; the Peterbilt picked up speed. Rocky feathered the brake treadle, snubbing the brakes lightly from time to time to bring the rig back to a safe speed without burning out the linings. The staccato bark of the engine brake reverberated off solid rock walls sounding like a machine gun. A sudden jolt from behind slammed their heads back against the restraints. Rocky checked the mirrors. The Kenworth's nose was obscured by Rocky's trailer as it pushed from behind, its engine roaring an accompaniment to the machine gun sound of the lead truck's engine brake.

Rocky depressed the foot brake a little farther as her truck picked up even more speed. The combination of engine brake and air brakes was no match for the force of the powerful Kenworth driving it downhill from behind like a locomotive.

"Doobie!" L.T. called out over the radio.

"I'm proceeding," he replied. "I'll get her off your ass. Move over to the right shoulder, I'll put her into the mountain."

Rocky eased over to run on the shoulder, dangerously close to the rock wall of the mountain. The other truck stayed with her, still pushing, still heating up her brakes, threatening to run her off the mountain if she let up for just a second. She tugged the chain to blast the air horns as she overtook a covered flatbed from the wrong side. Sweat trickled from her forehead. A quick glance in the mirror revealed the jagged rock wall glowing from the lights of the other truck behind. She clutched the wheel with all her strength, almost standing up now.

OVERDRIVE

"Get a grip, driver," called the flatbed hauler. "You're gonna kill somebody, you dumb ass. Burn your brakes out or is your road dope kickin' in?"

"Take the left lane, covered wagon!" Doobie shouted. "Move it now!"

The flatbed swung left. Doobie's Freightliner wheeled into the right lane, drew alongside the Kenworth and prepared to ram it from the side. The driver's window opened on Carla's truck. A hand emerged holding a gun. Its muzzle flashed. Doobie's windshield shattered.

"Tabernac!" he shouted. Grabbing the wheel with both hands he swung hard to the right. His body tensed and tightened like a banjo string, cringing in horror as the Freightliner rammed the side of the Kenworth. Sparks sprayed wildly from the grinding steel machines. "She's got a gun!" he cried over the radio. "That bitch is shooting at me!"

"Get her off us!" Rocky shouted back. "We haven't much left for brakes."

"When I ram her to the right, you go left." Doobie sideswiped the Kenworth again, trying to force it against the rock wall of the mountain. Something made a clunking sound in the front end of his truck. The steering wheel went loose in his hand. He steered to the right but the truck trailed left, its steering linkage broken. Doobie cruised dangerously close to the flatbed on his left. The Kenworth still appeared as if joined to the back of Rocky's truck. A sudden jolt from behind set him back in his seat. In the mirror Doobie spotted the lights of a black Mack that had just rammed his trailer from behind and was setting up to do it again.

"She's got help!" Doobie cried into the microphone. "And I've got no steering, eh."

Rocky watched the mirror as Doobie's truck began to slow and fall back slightly, the engine no longer driving it, but momentum refusing to allow it to slow much. As she looked on it was rammed again by the Mack. Suddenly, the Freightliner swerved left, barely missing the flatbed, crashed through the center barricade in a shower of sparks then crossed the southbound lanes, burst through the guardrail and plunged off the side of the mountain. Rocky screamed as its lights went out of sight.

"Call 911," she gasped. "Doobie just went off the mountain."

CHAPTER FIFTY-TWO

Rocky continued her deadly battle with the Kenworth behind, leaning over the steering wheel to swing the speeding Pete through the downhill curves, using both paved shoulders to avoid crashing into other vehicles. No matter which way she went, the Kenworth blindly followed, pushing like a runaway freight train. The two trucks careened down and around the mountain, perilously close to running out of control.

"We're going to make it," L.T. said, trying to sound calm. "It's a straight run to the bottom now, just don't run over anyone."

Rocky nodded but couldn't take her eyes off the road. As they flew past the exit at the Kentucky state line the road flattened for a few hundred yards. The Peterbilt began to lose momentum and slow. They checked the mirrors. The two killer trucks had disappeared. L.T. leaned out the window to look behind.

"They took the exit," he said. "They're gone." He let out a long, slow breath.

"Let's hope for good." She started to wheel the truck into the rest area at the Kentucky welcome center.

"Shouldn't we be putting some ground between us and them?" asked L.T.

"We've got to get help for Doobie."

"All we can do is report it," he said, pulling out his phone. "There's no way he could have survived that drop. I'm afraid we can't do a thing for our French-Canadian friend except thank him.

191

He probably saved our lives when they saw him go over. I guess they figured one life was payback enough for Marlin."

"Payback." She shook her head. "She's the one that deserves some payback. And now she's got help. That's sick." Rocky began to cry silently. "Poor Doobie." She kept the rig rolling through the rest area and back onto the highway. L.T. stared out the window, his fists clenched, wanting desperately to crush the evil monster in the fancy red, white and blue truck. Somehow, she had to be stopped.

"Poor Doobie," said L.T. "Poor Carla Sears when I track her down."

A couple of hours passed without further incident, giving the brakes time to cool, restoring their stopping power. CB reports kept crackling away about the spectacular wreck on the mountain. They called it a deadly game of chicken by road-crazed truckers who had finally snapped. Rocky and L.T. were running peacefully along near Richmond, Kentucky, working through steep hills again when their necks were suddenly wrenched backward by another heavy jolt from behind. They checked the mirrors simultaneously.

"Oh shit," said Rocky. "That must be the Mack back there."

"How can you tell?"

"Because the Kenworth is coming up on the left. Shit. They're getting ready to put us off the bridge at Clays Ferry."

"This wouldn't be a high bridge, would it?"

Rocky nodded. "We go off that span, we're as dead as Doobie."

Rocky's window shattered as a gun fired from the truck beside. Instinctively she ducked, then recovered and swerved left, striking the Kenworth with a grinding of metal and a shower of yellow sparks. The fancy rig backed off a bit, then began to approach again. The Mack rammed them again from the rear.

"That's it," said L.T. "Give me the flashlight."

She plucked it from beneath her seat and tossed it over. L.T. tucked it in his belt and reached for the door handle.

"What are you going to do?" asked Rocky.

"I'm not sure. Probably make it up as I go along. Just get me close to Carla's truck. It's time she saw the light."

He went out the door and climbed atop the hood of the speeding rig, then made his way to the roof of the sleeper. In a moment he crouched on the flat, aluminum top of the Great Dane trailer. L.T. struggled against the wind and the downhill angle to keep his balance on the careening trailer. Rocky eased the truck to the left, edging closer to Carla's Kenworth. L.T. looked rearward, saw the Mack setting up to ram again and made a frantic leap toward Carla's trailer a couple of feet away. He hit the smooth roof sliding and clawed at the aluminum roof, stopping just short of going off the far side. Staying low, he crept forward to the nose of the van and slid himself into a sitting position on top of the refrigeration unit, his legs dangling in front of it.

With a twist of the cap, he opened the flashlight, took out the batteries and let the rest fall. Two batteries fit into his shirt pocket. With the other two in his right hand, he leaned forward, his left fingers curled into the grillwork of the reefer to keep from falling. He popped two batteries down the red-hot right exhaust stack of the tractor, then quickly slid himself toward the left. The batteries exploded almost instantly, blasting shrapnel and sparks out the bottom of the exhaust pipe that ruptured the cylindrical aluminum fuel tank just below it. Flames began to lick upward at the side of the cab as the diesel fuel ignited. L.T. leaned left and dropped the remaining batteries into the other stack, ducking back on the roof as a second explosion boomed. Engine noise from now wide-open exhaust pipes roared, reaching a deafening level. Bright yellow flames rose up both sides of the star-spangled tractor. L.T. rolled backward on the roof of the trailer.

The explosions and flames caused Rocky to pull to the right to keep away from the rolling fireball. L.T. stared over at her trailer, getting farther away all the time. He glanced around, looking for another way off the screaming, fiery missile but knew that only death awaited if he jumped at that speed. He called out to Rocky, shouting with all the force he could muster, but could not even hear himself over the roar. He thought of trying to jump to the Mack behind as its driver shifted his focus from Rocky to Carla with the flames rising higher. But the Mack backed off too far.

Again, he judged the distance between him and Rocky's trailer. It seemed so far. He might make it only to have momentum carry him to his death off the far side. He looked again at the flames. The trailer began to sway from side to side as its driver tried to figure out how to escape a fiery death. To slow down or stop would certainly allow the flames to consume the cab. L.T. quickly tossed off his shoes and socks, stood to the left side of the speeding trailer, then took two quick steps and leaped. He landed roughly on his lower back and buttocks, his knees bent ahead of him, bare feet flat on the roof in an attempt to slow his slide. His hands reached out behind, fingers curled, feeling for the roof edge to stop himself. His fingers caught the drip rail, the weight of his body cut them to the bone but he stopped and hung onto the roof of Rocky's trailer. Rocky had begun to slow down, the two terrorist truckers no longer concentrating on her. As they rounded the curve just above Clays Ferry Carla's truck veered to the right, glanced off the sheer rock wall in a volley of sparks accompanying the flaming tanks. Missing the bridge cleanly it sailed out into the darkness, a burning flag hanging in mid-air a second, then plunged like a fiery comet to the rocky depths below, erupting into a yellow plume of flames.

Rocky was frantic but didn't dare stop harshly in case L.T. had somehow managed to make it back to her trailer. She continued to back off on the upgrade, finally rolling to a gentle stop. At almost the same moment, the passenger door swung open and L.T. climbed in, his bloody fingers cut to ribbons. Rocky set the parking brakes and leaped over to embrace him. Beau jumped up to lick his face.

"You're hurt," said Rocky.

"I'm okay," he replied. "Look." He pointed a bloody finger at the road ahead.

The flatbed that had been beside Doobie's truck when it went off the mountain pulled over and parked ahead of them. There on the trailer, clinging to a load strap, lay Doobie. He sat up and climbed down and said, "Tabernac. What a ride, eh?"

L.T. and Rocky both leaped out of the Peterbilt and ran to embrace him.

"How the hell did you get here? asked Rocky. "We saw you go off the mountain."

"Fuck that," said Doobie. "Like any good frog, I leaped. Lucky for me I caught a load strap and rode the flatbed down off the rock."

L.T. shook his head. "You're crazy, Doob."

"Me? I'm crazy? I see you jumping trailer to trailer, riding a fireball. I thought you went off Clays Ferry. You be crazy, too, monsieur." He looked at L.T.'s bloody hands. "You're hurt again. I can't take you nowhere. Better go back to being a cop. It's safer."

L.T. looked at Rocky. "We'll see."

Rocky nodded. "We'll see."

The black Mack took the next exit, swung around and entered the southbound ramp. Flames were still rising from the burning wreck below as the black truck slowly crossed the bridge. A crowd gathered, their vehicles lining the shoulders. The Mack rolled quietly past without anyone noticing. Down the road a few miles its driver finally pulled over in the darkness, her hands quivering.

"Oh, Jack," said Carla. "What have they done to you?"

CHAPTER FIFTY-THREE

A day and a half later L.T. and Rocky finally made it to Detroit, having to first spend time giving statements and explaining their actions to State Police and FBI agents. The interviews were conducted in the ER at hospital in Lexington while a surgeon stitched and dressed L.T.'s ragged fingers. Police and FBI were in agreement that the real Iceman Killer, Carla Sears, had died in a fiery crash in the Kentucky River. The fire became so intense that no human remains were ever recovered from the gorge.

Rocky pulled into the Stony Ridge Truck Stop south of Toledo. L.T. tugged his travel bag from the sleeper.

"Guess you're famous again," said Rocky. "If it all doesn't go to your head, I could still use a co-driver."

"I'd love to, Rocky, but I'd always feel like I was just running away from who I really am."

She just stared into his eyes with a half-smile.

"I don't know if I have a job anymore and I'll probably have to go crawling back to Ruby."

Rocky leaned over, took his bandaged hands and brought them to her face. She pulled him close and kissed him deeply. "When you sort things out," she said. "You know where to find me."

He smiled, hoisted his travel bag in a bandaged hand and climbed down from the yellow Peterbilt as Chet Connor pulled up in an OSHP patrol car. L.T. turned back to wave at Rocky just in

OVERDRIVE

time to see her wipe a tear from her cheek. He shut the truck door and she was rolling out of the truck stop, black smoke blowing from twin chrome stacks before he sat down in Chet's car.

The End

CPSIA information can be obtained
at www.ICGtesting.com
Printed in the USA
LVHW111509230223
740229LV00002B/82